GIVE
WAR
A
CHANCE

'He is wickedly good'
Sebastian Faulks, INDEPENDENT ON SUNDAY

'His sentences have the economy and timing of a proficient stand-up'
Laura Page, SUNDAY TELEGRAPH

'For the jokes alone, *Give War a Chance* is worth a read'
Jeremy Paxman, SUNDAY TIMES

'The US needs an unapologetic hedonist like P. J. O'Rourke on the literary scene, flashing two fingers at the forces behind random drug-testing and neutered lager . . . an exuberantly malevolent collection of journalese'
Douglas Kennedy, LITERARY REVIEW

'Not only the best title for years, but funnier than a billion politically correct comedies'
THE FACE

'A riveting read'

IE OUT

D1153856

P. J. O'ROURKE

EYEWITNESS
ACCOUNTS
OF MANKIND'S
STRUGGLE AGAINST
TYRANNY,
INJUSTICE AND
ALCOHOL-FREE BEER

GIVE
WAR
A
CHANCE

PICADOR

First published 1992 by The Atlantic Monthly Press, New York

First published in Great Britain 1992 by Picador
This edition published 1993 in Picador by Pan Books Limited
a division of Pan Macmillan Publishers Limited
Cavaye Place, London SW10 9PG
and Basingstoke

Associated companies throughout the world

ISBN 0 330 32842 5

9 8 7 6 5 4 3 2 1

A CIP catalogue record for this book is available from
the British Library

Phototypeset by Intype, London
Printed by Cox & Wyman Ltd, Reading

Like many men of my generation, I had an opportunity to give war a chance, and I promptly chickened out. I went to my draft physical in 1970 with a doctor's letter about my history of drug abuse. The letter was four and a half pages long with three and a half pages devoted to listing the drugs I'd abused. I was shunted into the office of an Army psychiatrist who, at the end of a forty-five-minute interview with me, was pounding the desk and shouting, 'You're fucked up! You don't belong in the Army!' He was certainly right on the first count and possibly right on the second. Anyway, I didn't have to go. But that, of course, meant someone else had to go in my place. I would like to dedicate this book to him.

I hope you got back in one piece, fellow. I hope you were more use to your platoon mates than I would have been. I hope you're rich and happy now. And in 1971, when somebody punched me in the face for being a long-haired peace creep, I hope that was you.

CONTENTS

CONTENTS

ACKNOWLEDGMENTS

'The Death of Communism', 'Return of the Death of Communism, Part III', and most of the Gulf War section of this book originally appeared in *Rolling Stone*, where I am the 'Foreign Affairs Desk Chief', a title given to me because 'Middle-Aged Drunk' didn't look good on business cards. I would like to thank Jann Wenner and the staff of *Rolling Stone*, especially Bob Wallace, Eric Etheridge and Robert Vare for good editing, better ideas and best paychecks.

Although the Gulf War dispatches appeared in *Rolling Stone*, it was ABC Radio that actually sent me to Saudi Arabia. The General Manager of News Operations, my friend John Lyons, called me from Dhahran and said, 'I noticed your bylines on the Kuwait invasion story were Jordan and the UAE, and this tells me you haven't been able to get a Saudi visa.' John got me one and got me a job, too (my first real one since 1980), doing commentary for his radio network. The 'Gulf Diary' entries and much of the material in the *Rolling Stone* dispatches are drawn from my radio pieces. I know nothing about radio, and John was a patient boss – though his patience was sorely tried when I wound up, briefly, as the only ABC Radio reporter in liberated Kuwait City and was sending back live reports such as: 'Uh, uh, uh, uh . . . oh my gosh, blown-up tanks'. Many thanks go to

John and to the equally patient real ABC Radio reporters in the Gulf, Linda Albin, Chuck Taylor and Bob Schmidt.

'Return of the Death of Communism', 'Fiddling While Africa Starves', 'The Deep Thoughts of Lee Iacocca', 'The Very Deep Thoughts of Jimmy and Rosalynn Carter' and 'Mordred Had a Point – Camelot Revisited' all appeared in the *American Spectator*, as did 'Notes Toward a Blacklist for the 1990s'. This last was expanded, with the aid of the *Spectator*'s readers, into a book-length proscription called *The New Enemies List*. Copies are available from *The American Spectator*, P.O. Box 549, Arlington, VA 22216. My thanks to R. Emmett Tyrrell, Jr, Wladyslaw Pleszczynski, Andrew Ferguson and the rest of the staff of that fine publication.

'Second Thoughts About the 1960s' was originally a speech, given in October 1987 at the Second Thoughts conference in Washington, DC. Second Thoughts was a gathering of former New Leftists and other people who had successfully recovered from the sixties. The conference was put together by Peter Collier and David Horowitz, and we all had a great time chastising our former selves. Part of my speech was published in the *New Republic*, then under the brilliant (even if he does call himself a liberal) editorship of Michael Kinsley. The entire text was printed in the book *Second Thoughts*, edited by Collier and Horowitz and published by Madison Books (Lanham, Md) in 1989.

The Second Thoughts conference was organized with the help of Jim Denton, Director of the National Forum Foundation, one of Washington's more thoughtful think tanks. The National Forum Foundation has worked hard and even successfully to aid pro-liberty forces in Central America and Eastern Europe. It was Jim Denton who convinced me to go to Nicaragua for the 1990 elections. Jim even went so far as to claim Violeta Chamorro might win.

'A Serious Problem' was commissioned by the intelligent and beautiful Shelley Wanger, then Articles Editor of *House and Garden*. But Ms Wanger left, *House and Garden* became *HG* and my piece was judged to contain too few photographs of celebrity bed linen.

'Studying for Our Drug Test' appeared in *Playboy*, assigned by sagacious Articles Editor John Rezek. 'The Two-Thousand-Year-Old US Middle East Policy Expert' was published in *Inquiry* at the behest of its excellent Managing Editor, Jack Shafer. 'An Argument in Favor of Automobiles vs Pedestrians' saw print in *Car and Driver* when that doughty publication was being run by the as-doughty or doughtier David E. Davis, Jr. And 'Sex with Dr Ruth' came out in *Vanity Fair*, Executive Literary Editor Wayne Lawson being the only person on earth who could convince me to go see Dr Ruth, let alone admit it later.

Additional thanks are due to Morgan Entrekin, my editor and publisher, who paid me again for all these articles even though I'd been paid for them already, and to Bob Dattila, my agent, who made Morgan do that. And I must sincerely – though sincerity is not my forte – thank my wife. She had been my wife for only a month when the air war started in the Gulf and I headed there for the duration. She didn't cry, she didn't complain, she didn't let the car insurance lapse. And, when she heard about the way I almost set off a booby trap by fooling around with a box of Iraqi ammunition, she said – in even, measured tones – those words which elucidate so well the content and the style of all my journalism work: 'P.J., that was really stupid.'

' . . . and from the nothingness of good works, she passed to the somethingness of ham and toast with great cheerfulness.'

– Charles Dickens
BARNABY RUDGE

HUNTING THE VIRTUOUS – AND HOW TO CLEAN AND SKIN THEM

This book is a collection of articles about – if I may be excused for venturing upon a large theme – the battle against evil. Not that I meant to do anything so grand. I was just writing magazine pieces, trying to make a living, and evil is good copy.

Various types of evil are battled here. Some are simple. Iraq's invasion of Kuwait is a case of bad men doing wrong things for wicked reasons. This is the full-sized or standard purebred evil and is easily recognized even by moral neophytes. Other malignities – drugs in America, famine in Africa and everything in the Levant – are more complex. When combating those evils people sometimes have trouble deciding whom to shoot.

Anyway, it's a book about evil – evil ends, evil means, evil effects and causes. In a compilation of modern journalism there's nothing surprising about that. What does surprise me, on rereading these articles, is how much of the evil was authored or abetted by liberals.

Now liberals are people I had been accustomed to thinking of as daffy, not villainous. Getting their toes caught in their sandal straps, bumping their heads on wind chimes – how much trouble could they cause, even in a full-blown cultural-diversity frenzy? (I mean if Europeans didn't discover North America, how'd we all get here?) But every iniquity in this book is traceable to bad thinking or bad government. And liberals have been vigorous cheerleaders for both.

'Liberal' is, of course, one of those fine English words, like lady, gay and welfare, which has been spoiled by special pleading. When I say *liberals* I certainly don't mean openhanded individuals or tolerant persons or even Big Government Democrats. I mean people who are excited that one per cent of the profits of Ben & Jerry's ice-cream goes to promote world peace.

The principal feature of contemporary American liberalism is sanctimoniousness. By loudly denouncing all bad things – war and hunger and date rape – liberals testify to their own terrific goodness. More important, they promote themselves to membership in a self-selecting elite of those who care deeply about such things. People who care a lot are naturally superior to we who don't care any more than we have to. By virtue of this superiority the caring have a moral right to lead the nation. It's a kind of natural aristocracy, and the wonderful thing about this aristocracy is that you don't have to be brave, smart, strong or even lucky to join it, you just have to be liberal.* Kidnapping the moral high ground also serves to inflate liberal ranks. People who are, in fact, just kindhearted are told that because they care, they must be liberals, too.

Liberals hate wealth, they say, on grounds of economic injustice – as though prosperity were a pizza, and if I have too many slices, you're left with nothing but a Domino's box to feed your family. Even Castro and Kim Il Sung know this to be nonsense. Any rich man does more for society than all the jerks pasting VISUALIZE WORLD PEACE bumper stickers on their cars. The worst leech of a merger and acquisitions lawyer making $500,000 a year will, even if he cheats on his taxes, put $100,000 into the public coffers. That's $100,000 worth of education, charity or US

*It was that talented idiot Percy Bysshe Shelley who first posited this soggy oligarchy when he said, 'Poets are the unacknowledged legislators of the world.' Modern liberals are no poets, however, and are hardly satisfied with legislating in the unacknowledged manner. Today's liberals love politics as much as they love disappearing rain forests, homelessness and hate crimes, because politics is one more way to achieve power without merit or risk.

Marines. And the Marine Corps does more to promote world peace than all the Ben & Jerry's ice-cream ever made.

Liberals actually hate wealth because they hate all success. They hate success especially, of course, when it's achieved by other people, but sometimes they even hate the success they achieve themselves. What's the use of belonging to a self-selecting elite if there's a real elite around? Liberals don't like any form of individual achievement. And if there has to be some, they prefer the kind that cannot be easily quantified – 'the achievement of Winnie Mandela' for example. Also wealth is, for most people, the only honest and likely path to liberty. With money comes power over the world. Men are freed from drudgery, women from exploitation. Businesses can be started, homes built, communities formed, religions practiced, educations pursued. But liberals aren't very interested in such real and material freedoms. They have a more innocent – not to say toddlerlike – idea of freedom. Liberals want the freedom to put anything into their mouths, to say bad words and to expose their private parts in art museums.

That liberals aren't enamoured of real freedom may have something to do with responsibility – that cumbersome backpack which all free men have to lug on life's aerobic nature hike. The second item in the liberal creed, after self-righteousness, is unaccountability. Liberals have invented whole college majors – psychology, sociology, women's studies – to prove that nothing is anybody's fault. No one is fond of taking responsibility for his actions, but consider how much you'd have to hate free will to come up with a political platform that advocates killing unborn babies but not convicted murderers. A callous pragmatist might favour abortion *and* capital punishment. A devout Christian would sanction neither. But it takes years of therapy to arrive at the liberal point of view.

Since we're not in control of ourselves, we are all vulnerable to victimization by whatever *is* in control. (Liberals are vague about this, but it's probably white male taxpayers or the Iran–Contra conspiracy). Liberals are fond of victims and seek them wherever they go. The more victimized the better – the best victims being too ignorant and addled to challenge their benefactors. This is why animal rights is such an excellent liberal issue. Not even a Democratic presidential candidate is as ignorant and addled as a dead laboratory rat.

The search for victims of injustice to pester explains why liberals won't leave minorities alone. 'The minority is always right,' said that pesky liberal Ibsen. And, when it comes to minorities, there is none greater – or, as it were, lesser – than that ultimate of all minorities, the self. Here the liberal truly comes into his own. There is nothing more mealy-mouthed, bullying, irresponsible and victimized than a well-coddled self, especially if it belongs to a liberal.

Liberal self-obsession is manifested in large doses of quack psychoanalysis, crank spiritualism, insalubrious health fads and helpless self-help seminars. The liberal makes grim attempts to hold on to his youth – fussing with his hair, his wardrobe, his speech and even his ideology in an attempt to retain the perfect solipsism of adolescence. He has a ridiculous and egotistical relationship with God, by turns denying He exists and hiding in His skirts. Either way – as God's special friend or as the highest form of sentient life on the planet – liberal self-importance is increased. The liberal is continually angry, as only a self-important man can be, with his civilization, his culture, his country and his folks back home. His is an infantile world view. At the core of liberalism is the spoiled child – miserable, as all spoiled children are, unsatisfied, demanding, ill-disciplined, despotic and useless. Liberalism is a philosophy of sniveling brats.

There! It was good to get that off my chest. Now that I've had my say, however, you may be wondering – don't I sometimes get called a Nazi? Yes, name-calling, in which conservatives such as myself are so loath to indulge, is a favourite tactic of the liberals. I have often been called a Nazi, and, although it is unfair, I don't let it bother me. I don't let it bother me for one simple reason. No one has *ever* had a fantasy about being tied to a bed and sexually ravished by someone dressed as a liberal.

THE BIRTH, AND SOME OF THE AFTERBIRTH, OF FREEDOM

THE
DEATH
Berlin, ## OF
November 1989 # COMMUNISM

A week after the surprise-party opening of East Germany's borders people were still gathering at the Berlin Wall, smiling at each other, drinking champagne and singing bits of old songs. There was no sign of the letdown which every sublime experience is supposed to inspire. People kept coming back just to walk along the freshly useless ramparts. They came at all sorts of hours, at lunch, dawn, three in the morning. Every possible kind of person was on promenade in the narrow gutter beside the concrete eyesore: wide hausfraus, kids with lavender hair, New Age goofs, drunk war vets in wheelchairs, video-burdened tourists, Deadheads, extravagant gays, toughs become all well-behaved, art students forgetting to look cool and bored, business tycoons gone loose and weepy, people so ordinary they defied description and, of course, members of the East German proletariat staring in surprise – as they stared in surprise at everything – at this previously central fact of their existence.

Even West Berlin's radicals joined the swarms. West Berlin had the most dogmatic agitators this side of Peru's Shining Path, but that was before 9 November. Near the restored Reichstag building I overheard a group of lefties amicably discussing nuclear strategy with a half dozen off-duty US GIs.

'Ja, you see, tactical capability mit der cruise missiles after all vas not der Soviet primary concern . . . '

'Sure, man, but what about second-strike capability? Wow, if we hadn't had that . . . '

All in the past tense. A British yob, who certainly should have been off throttling Belgians at a football match, came up to me apropos of nothing and said, 'I fucking 'ad to see this, right? I 'itched 'ere from London and got these chunks off the wall. You think I can't pay for the fucking ferry ride back with these? Right!'

At the Brandenburg Gate the East German border guards had shooed the weekend's noisy celebrators off the Wall. But the guards weren't carrying guns anymore and were beginning to acknowledge their audience and even ham it up a bit. Somebody offered a champagne bottle to a guard and he took a lively swig. Somebody else offered another bottle with a candle in it, and the guard set the candle on the wall and used a plastic cup to make a shield around the flame.

The people in the crowd weren't yelling or demanding anything. They weren't waiting for anything to happen. They were present from sheer glee at being alive in this place at this time. They were there to experience the opposite of the existential anguish which has been the twentieth century's designer mood. And they were happy with the big, important happiness that – the Declaration of Independence reminds us – is everybody's, even a Communist's, unalienable right to pursue.

The world's most infamous symbol of oppression had been rendered a tourist attraction overnight. Poland's political prisoners were now running its government. Bulgaria's leadership had been given the Order of the Boot. The Hungarian Communist Party wouldn't answer to its name. Three hundred thousand Czechs were tying a tin can to the Prague Politburo's tail. And the Union of Soviet Socialist Republics was looking disunified, unsoviet and not as socialist as it used to. What did it mean? The Commies didn't seem to know. The Bush administration didn't either. And you can be certain that members of the news media did not have a clue. Ideology, politics and journalism,

4

which luxuriate in failure, are impotent in the face of hope and joy.

I booked a hotel room in East Berlin. When I arrived at the West Berlin airport a taxi dispatcher said the border crossings were so busy that I'd better take the subway to the other side. The train was filled with both kinds of Berliners, and stepping through the car doors was like walking into a natural history museum diorama of Dawn Man and his modern relations. The Easterners looked like Pleistocene proto-Germans, as yet untouched by the edifying effects of Darwinian selection. West Germans are tall, pink, pert and orthodontically corrected, with hands, teeth and hair as clean as their clothes and clothes as sharp as their looks. Except for the fact that they all speak English pretty well, they're indistinguishable from Americans. East Germans seem to have been hunching over cave fires a lot. They're short and thick with sallow, lardy fat, and they have Khrushchev warts. There's something about Marxism that brings out warts – the only kind of growth this economic system encourages.

As the train ran eastward, West Berliners kept getting off and East Berliners kept getting on until, passing under the Wall itself, I was completely surrounded by the poor buggers and all the strange purchases they'd made in the west. It was mostly common, trivial stuff, things the poorest people would have already in any free country – notebook paper, pliers and screwdrivers, corn flakes and, especially, bananas. For all the meddling the Communist bloc countries have done in banana republics, they still never seem to be able to get their hands on any actual bananas.

The East Berliners had that glad but dazed look which you see on Special Olympics participants when they're congratulated by congressmen. The man sitting next to me held a West German tabloid open to a photo of a healthy fräulein without her clothes. He had that picture fixed with a gaze to make stout Cortez on a peak in Darien into a blinking, purblind myope.

At the Friedrichstrasse station in East Berlin, passport examination was perfunctory and the customs inspection, a wave of the hand. I walked outside into a scene of shocking, festive bustle. Though, to the uninitiated, I don't suppose it would look like much – just squat, gray crowds on featureless streets. But there are never crowds in East Berlin. And the crowds had shopping bags. There's nothing to shop for in East Berlin and no bags in which to put the stuff you can't buy. Taxi drivers saw my luggage and began shouting, 'You want taxi?!' 'Taxi, ja?!' Imagine shouting that your services are for hire in East Berlin. Imagine shouting. Imagine services. I heard laughter, chatting, even giggles. I saw a cop directing traffic with bold and dramatic flourishes. I saw border guards smile. It was a regular Carnival in Rio by East Berlin standards. And, the most amazing thing of all, there was jaywalking.

I had been in East Berlin three years before. And I had been standing on a corner of a perfectly empty Karl-Marx-Allee waiting for the light to change. All Germans are good about obeying traffic signals but pre-1989 East Germans were religious. If a bulb burned out they'd wait there until the state withered away and true communism arrived. So I was standing among about a dozen East Germans, meaning to follow the custom of the country, but my mind wandered and without thinking I stepped out into the street against the light. They all followed me. Then I realized I'd walked into the path of a speeding army truck. I froze in confusion. They froze in confusion. Finally I jumped back on the curb. And they did too, but not until I'd jumped first.

In 1986 I'd come through the border at Checkpoint Charlie, and getting in was a dreary and humiliating experience similar to visiting a brother-in-law in prison. There was much going through pairs of electrically locked doors and standing before counters fronted with bulletproof glass while young dolts in uniforms gave you the fish-eye. There were an inordinate number of 'NO EXIT!' signs, and I remember thinking the exclamation points were a nice touch.

You had to exchange twenty-five perfectly good West German marks, worth about fifty cents apiece, for twenty-five perfectly useless East German marks, worth nothing. I thought I'd see how fast I could blow my stack of East marks on the theory that the test of any society's strength and vigor is how quickly it Handi-Vacs your wallet.

I walked to Unter den Linden, old Berlin's Champs Elysées. The city was empty feeling, no construction noise, no music, no billboards or flashing lights. There were plenty of people around but they all seemed to be avoiding one another like patrons at a pornographic movie theater and, although it was a beautiful spring day, the East Berliners were moving with their shoulders hunched and heads turned down as though they were walking in the rain. The women were frumps but the men bore an odd resemblance to trendy New Yorkers. They had the same pallor and mixing-bowl haircuts. They wore the same funny, tight high-water pants with black clown shoes as big as rowboats and the same ugly 1950s geometric-patterned shirts buttoned to the neck. Except the East Berlin guys weren't kidding. This wasn't a style. These were their clothes.

Unter den Linden's six lanes served only a few deformed East German Wartburg sedans and some midget Trabant cars. The Trabants had two-cycle engines and made a sound like a coffee can full of steel washers and bees. They looked like they were made of plastic because they were. Other than that the traffic was mostly blimp-sized double-length articulated buses progressing down the vacant avenue at the speed of Dutch Elm disease.

The store windows were full of goods, however: a fifty-bottle pyramid of Rumanian berry liqueur, a hundred Russian nesting dolls, a whole enormous display devoted entirely to blue plastic toothbrushes with the bristles already falling out. The huge Centrum department store smelled as though the clothes were made from wet dogs. The knit dresses were already unraveling on their hangers. The sweaters were pilling on the shelves. The raincoats were made out of what looked like vinyl wallpaper. And there were thirty or forty people in line to buy anything, anything at all, that was for sale.

I went to a bar in the showplace Palace of the Republic. It took me thirty minutes to be waited on although there were two bartenders and only five other people in the place. The two bartenders were pretty busy washing out the bar's highball glass. I was amazed to see 'Manhattan' listed on the drink menu and ordered it and should have known better. There was some kind of alcohol, but definitely not whiskey, in the thing and the sweet vermouth had been replaced with ersatz sloe gin.

Next, I stood in line for half an hour to see what Marxism could do to street-vendor pizza. It did not disappoint. The word *cottony* is sometimes used to describe bad pizza dough, but there was every reason to believe this pizza was really made of the stuff, or maybe a polyester blend. The slice – more accurately, lump – had no tomato whatsoever and was covered in a semiviscous imitation mozzarella, remarkably uncheeselike even for a coal-tar by-product. Then there was the sausage topping. One bite brought a flood of nostalgia. Nobody who's been through a fraternity initiation will ever forget this taste, this smell. It was dog food.

I went back to Checkpoint Charlie. You weren't allowed to take East German money out of the country. I don't know why. It's not like there was anything you could do with it in the west. The bills are too small for house-training puppies. But East Germany was so total in its totalitarianism that everything was banned which wasn't compulsory. Anyway, when I went through customs a dour official in his early twenties said, 'Have you any currency of the German Democratic Republic?'

'Nope,' I said. 'I spent it all.'

He looked skeptical, as well he might have. 'Empty pockets, *bitte*,' he ordered. I had twenty-one marks left over.

'Well, I'm coming back tomorrow,' I said.

His expression changed for a moment to boyish amazement. 'You *are*?' He resumed his governmental frown. 'This once I will allow you to retain these currencies because you are coming back tomorrow,' he said and rolled his eyes.

I did come back and this time couldn't find anything at all to spend money on. The only excitement available in East Berlin seemed to be opening the subway car doors and getting off the train before it came to a complete halt. But I couldn't figure out how to pay the subway fare so I couldn't even spend my money on this. I walked back toward Checkpoint Charlie with forty-six marks in my pocket. Then I did something my capitalist soul had never allowed me to do before in my life. I crumpled up money and threw it in a garbage can.

There was no question of throwing money away on my 1989 visit to East Berlin. The glimmering new Grand Hotel, standing on that very corner where the garbage can had been, accepted only hard currency. In return you got food you could swallow and Johnnie Walker Scotch at the bar (although something described as 'cod liver in oil' still lurked on the restaurant menu).

There had been changes for the regular citizens of East Berlin as well. There were three or four times as many shops on the streets, some with pseudo-boutique names like 'Medallion', 'Panda' and 'Joker'. The stuff for sale was awful enough, but there was more of it. Thus at least half the law of supply and demand was being obeyed – if something's lousy, it's always available. The first line-up of shoppers I saw turned out to be waiting for an antique shop to open. The new Wartburg 353 models even had styling – not much styling and that borrowed from 1960s Saabs, but styling none the less.

However, the real change was the lack of fear, a palpable physical absence like letting go of your end of a piano. My note-taking – which in 1986 would have sent passers-by scuttling like roaches surprised in a kitchen – now went unremarked. American reporters were all over the place, of course. And in every hotel lobby and café you could hear East Germans griping loudly to the reporters while the reporters loudly explained how all this was feeling to the people of East Germany.

There were pictures everywhere of the new East German leader, Egon Krenz, just as there'd been pictures everywhere of the old East German leader, Erich Honecker. But these weren't the lifted chin, stalwart forward-looker vanguarding the masses photos. Egon – who resembles a demented nephew of Danny Thomas's – was shown spreading hugs around, tousling toddler mop-tops and doing the grip-and-grin at various humble functions. He was politicking, plain and simple. The Commies didn't quite have it right yet: they take office and *then* they run for it. But they're trying.

Personally I missed the old East Berlin. The only thing East Germany ever had going for it was a dramatic and sinister *film noir* atmosphere. When you passed through Checkpoint Charlie the movie footage seemed to switch to black and white. Steam rose from manhole covers. Newspapers blew down wet, empty streets. You'd turn your trench coat collar up, hum a few bars of 'Lili Marlene' and say to yourself, 'This is me in East Berlin.'

That's gone now and the place is revealed for what it's really been all along, just a screwed-up poor country with a dictatorship. The dictatorship part is understandable, but how the Commies managed to make a poor country out of a nation full of Germans is a mystery. The huge demonstrations that had shaken East Germany for the past several months had one characteristic which distinguished them from all other huge demonstrations in history – they never began until after work. I went to one of these at Humboldt University. The students were demanding economics courses. It was hard to reconcile this with my own memories of student protest. We were demanding free dope for life.

The students were also protesting the opening of the Wall. Not that they were against it. But they were furious that the East German government might think this was all it had to do. One picket sign showed a caricature of East Berlin's party boss, Gunther Schabowski, naked with a banana stuck in every orifice and a balloon reading, 'Free at last!' No one made any attempt to break up the rally. Soldiers and police were there, but they were applauding the speakers.

Even though the guard dogs and the machine-gun nests were gone, the east side of the Berlin Wall was still pristine, smooth whitewashed pre-cast reinforced-concrete slabs a foot thick and ten feet high and separated from the rest of the city by thirty yards of police. On the west side, the Wall was in your face and covered with graffiti paint as thick as ravioli.

I went out Checkpoint Charlie – with nobody worrying over

what I might do with my East German marks – and turned right on Zimmer Strasse, what Berliners call 'Wall Street' because the Wall runs along the old curbstone, leaving only a sidewalk in front of the West Berlin buildings. There was a steely, rhythmic noise that, for a moment, I thought might be some new Kraft-werk-style European synthesizer music (Berliners are horribly up-to-date with that sort of thing). But it was the sound of hundreds of people going at the Wall with hammers, chisels, picks, sledges, screwdrivers and even pocket knives. The chip-ping and flaking had progressed in a week until long, mouse-gnawed-looking ellipses were appearing between the slabs with daylight and occasional glimpses of East German border guards visible on the other side. I saw thirty schoolchildren on a class excursion with their teacher, all beating the Wall in unison with rocks, sticks and anything that came to hand.

I talked to a man in his sixties who was going along the Wall with a rucksack and a geologist's hammer. He'd escaped from the East in 1980. He'd been in prison over there for his political opinions. He gestured at the layers of spray-painting, the hundreds of symbols, slogans and messages ranging from John Lennon quotes to 'Fuck the IRA'. 'I want one piece of every color,' he said.

A twenty-year-old West German named Heiko Lemke was attacking the Wall with a set of professional stonemason's tools. In two days he'd made a hole big enough to pass a house cat through, even though the police had twice confiscated his cold chisels – the West German police. During a one-minute breather Lemke said he was an engineering student, a supporter of the Christian Democratic Party, didn't want history to repeat itself and was going to come back to the Wall on the weekend with some serious equipment.

Two American teenagers, Neville Finnis and Daniel Sheire, from Berlin's English-language JFK high school, were attempting to rip the top off one section of the Wall with their bare hands. The Wall is capped with six-foot-long two-hundred-pound half pipes cast in ferroconcrete. These need to be lifted nearly a foot in the air before their edges clear the cement slab and they can

11

be heaved to the ground. Neville and Daniel straddled the wall, in postures that would bring dollar signs to the eyes of any hernia surgeon, and lifted. When that didn't work, two more JFK students got up on the Wall and lifted Neville and Daniel while Neville and Daniel lifted the half-pipe. 'Go for it! Go for it!' they yelled at each other. It was an American, rather than a scientific or methodical, approach. The half-pipe landed with a great thump. The political message was clear to all the JFK students. 'Yeah!' shouted one. 'Let's sell it!'

The East German border guards didn't interfere. Instead they came up to openings in the Wall and made V signs and posed for photographs. One of them even stuck his hand through and asked would somebody please give him a piece of concrete to keep as a souvenir.

The hand of that border guard – that disembodied, palm-up, begging hand . . . I looked at that and I began to cry.

I really didn't understand before that moment, I didn't realize until just then – we won. The Free World won the Cold War. The fight against life-hating, soul-denying, slavish communism – which has shaped the world's politics this whole wretched century – was over.

The tears of victory ran down my face – and the snot of victory did too because it was a pretty cold day. I was blubbering like a lottery winner.

All the people who had been sent to gulags, who'd been crushed in the streets of Budapest, Prague and Warsaw, the soldiers who'd died in Korea and my friends and classmates who had been killed in Vietnam – it meant something now. All the treasure that we in America had poured into guns, planes, Star Wars and all the terrifying A-bombs we'd had to build and keep – it wasn't for nothing.

And I didn't get it until just then, when I saw that border guard's hand. And I think there are a lot of people who haven't gotten it yet. Our own President Bush seems to regard the events in Eastern Europe as some kind of odd dance craze or something. When I got back to the United States, I was looking through the magazines and newspapers and it seemed that all I saw were editorial writers pulling long faces about 'Whither a United Germany' and 'Whence America's Adjustments to the New Realities in Europe'. Is that the kind of noise people were making in Times Square on V-E Day?

I say, Shut-up you egghead flap-gums. We've got the whole rest of history to sweat the small stuff. And those discredited peace creeps, they can zip their soup-coolers, too. They think Mikhail Gorbachev is a visionary? Yeah, he's a visionary. Like Hirohito was after Nagasaki. We won. And let's not let anybody forget it. We the people, the free and equal citizens of democracies, we living exemplars of the Rights of Man tore a new asshole in International Communism. Their wall is breached. Their gutstring is busted. The rot of their dead body politic fills the nostrils of the earth with a glorious stink. We cleaned the clock of Marxism. We mopped the floor with them. We ran the Reds through the wringer and hung them out to dry. The privileges of liberty and the sanctity of the individual went out and whipped butt.

And the best thing about our victory is the way we did it – not just with ICBMs and Green Berets and aid to the Contras. Those things were important, but in the end we beat them with Levi 501 jeans. Seventy-two years of communist indoctrination and propaganda was drowned out by a three-ounce Sony Walkman. A huge totalitarian system with all its tanks and guns, gulag camps and secret police has been brought to its knees because nobody wants to wear Bulgarian shoes. They may have had the soldiers and the warheads and the fine-sounding ideology that suckered the college students and nitwit Third Worlders, but we had all the fun. Now they're lunch, and we're number one on the planet.

It made me want to do a little sack dance right there in the Cold War's end zone. We're the best! We're the greatest! The only undefeated socio-economic system in the league! I wanted to get up on the Wall and really rub it in: 'Taste the ash-heap of history, you Bolshie nose-wipes!' But there was nobody to jeer at. Everyone over there was in West Berlin watching Paula Abdul videos.

	DEMOCRACY
	IN
Paraguay,	**ITS**
April 1989	**DIAPERS**

Asunción, Paraguay, is farther from New York than Moscow. Not that it matters how far away a thing is if you don't know where it's at. My friends couldn't quite place Paraguay. Most of them thought Paraguay was where Uruguay is. Others thought it was between Colombia and Peru. And one young lady – a college graduate – had it confused with Papua New Guinea. Paraguay is the difference between a B and a B– on a geography exam, or would be if people took geography anymore, which they don't. United States diplomats privately refer to Paraguay as 'the Tibet of South America'. (Though the mystical religion of Paraguay has never caught on with New Age types because there's no such thing as Tantric Catholicism.) Paraguay is nowhere and it's famous for nothing.

Or almost nothing. Paraguay has been a popular hiding place for Nazi war criminals such as Josef Mengele because when a Nazi war criminal hides in Paraguay everybody goes looking for him in Uruguay and Papua New Guinea. And Paraguay used to have this classic of a tinpot dictator, General Alfredo Stroessner, who'd been *El Sleazo Caudillo* since 1954. They don't make them like the Stroess anymore. Stroessner was so old and nasty that if Latin America were a soap opera – and some argue it is – you could cast him as the cold, disciplinarian dad that young, sensitive, caring Augusto Pinochet rebels against. Stroessner was all wizened and drooly and spent his days reviewing troops, sitting in the stands in a uniform copied off the cover of *Sgt Pepper's Lonely Hearts Club Band* and wearing one of those great big general hats with two pounds of brass macaroni on the brim which would fall down over his eyes while he snoozed to the lulling sound of goose steps.

In Latin America – as in any good soap opera – the worse a situation is, the longer it lasts. So it came as a surprise and a shock to everyone when Man-Mummy Stroessner got a *coup* in the *état* from his own army chief of staff, the porky, affable and corrupt General Andrés Rodríguez.

General Rodríguez promptly called for elections. Elections are a fad in the developing world for the same reason portable tape decks are a fad in the inner city. Elections and tape decks both make a lot of noise. They both attract attention. And having an election, like having a tape deck, is crucial to achieving job skills and social justice.

Suddenly Paraguay was news. Page 8, one-paragraph, wire-service-filler-item-news, but news. Dozens, okay, one dozen American reporters flew to Asunción. And US diplomats began privately referring to Paraguay as 'the *former* Tibet of South America'.

I was not prepared to love Paraguay. I was not prepared to do anything but upchuck and die after the eight-hour night flight from Miami on an Air Paraguay DC-8 older than most second wives that flew through the center of five Dr Frankenstein-your-lab-is-on-the-phone lightning storms and aboard which I was served a dinner of roast softball in oleo. But as we shuddered down out of the atmosphere dawn cut loose with that annoying beauty which I never get to see except when I'm sick to my stomach from some life disruption. Mists soft and transparent as excuses flapped across pastures the color of crap-table felt. Out on the tarmac the air was cool, moist and floral – God's Wash'n' Dri. The Paraguayan customs inspection was a most informal formality. The taxi cab, an Alfa-Romeo sedan, was old and dented but rubbed to a shine. And the taxi driver was the only taxi driver on earth able to drive from an international airport to a downtown hotel without opening his yap.

There was nothing Latin American about the ride into Asunción, no litter, no shanty towns, no remains of horrendous bus wrecks. Traffic stayed in its lane and obeyed the posted speed limit – phenomena unusual enough to trigger a police investigation in most places south of the Rio Grande. Every street was lined with palms and frangipanis and pink-blossoming bottle trees. Every street was also lined with children going cheerfully, even willingly, to school. Each face was scrubbed, each head combed just so. Uniform blouses were as white and stiff as typing paper. The little boys wore shorts. Bigger boys wore ties with all-thumb four-in-hand knots. Teenage girls moved with the first wiggles of self-consciousness inside their modest frocks. I felt a completely unprofessional sense of cheery peace descending upon me. This is *tranquilo*, a very Paraguayan state of mind. The hotel was good. The breakfast was better. I poured myself a small restorative from the mini-bar and slept until siesta. Then I got up and took a nap.

Journalists aren't supposed to praise things. It's a violation of work rules almost as serious as buying drinks with our own money or absolving the CIA of something. Not only that, but if a journalist shows a facility for praise he's liable to be offered a job in public relations or advertising and the next thing you know he's got a big office, a huge salary and is living in a fine home with a lovely wife and swell kids – another career blown to hell. So I'm wrestling with the angel of reportage here, fully aware that good news is no news, but I can't help myself. Even a person with the soul of a foreign correspondent has to like something sometime, and I like Paraguay.

Asunción is a city with about the same population as Austin, Texas. It is built on unassuming hills overlooking a New York Harbor-sized backwater of the River Paraguay. This is the third largest river in the western hemisphere and even here, one thousand miles from its mouth on the Atlantic, its waters are so broad and calm that Paraguay hardly seems to be a landlocked country. You'd think you were in some balmy coast, Florida maybe. Paraguay's climate is almost identical to Florida's but more comfortable since nobody has to wear a giant mouse costume to make a living.

Zoning is not a concept hereabouts, so Asunción is a pleasant jumble of buildings – office towers next to mansions next to little shops next to big hotels. Some of the architecture is the Río de la Plata Argentine type, a distant cousin of the Taco Bell school. And the newer buildings are that kind of modernistic which is looking so old-fashioned these days. But most of Asunción was built around the turn of the century in what's called the 'academic style', where elements of the classical, baroque and beaux-arts were gathered higgledy-piggledy and set down hodgepodge in painted stucco instead of carved stone. It's a kind of imitation European façade I've only seen in one other place – Russia. The design influences are French and Italian but the effect is subtropical Leningrad, a very relaxed subtropical Leningrad.

Asunción is so relaxed that there are no traffic lights or stop signs at the downtown intersections. Cars just noodle up to the corners and wave one another by. I accidentally ran a road block by the Presidential Palace and the soldiers shrugged. The whole city closes, firmly and without exception, at noon. People go out and have a few drinks and a big lunch. Then they go home, make love, doze, take a shower, change clothes and return to work – refreshed to the point of exhaustion – at three. Stores and offices stay open until seven. Or six. Four-thirty, anyway.

Paraguay is a poor country. Twice as poor as Mexico, if you believe in statistics. Yet the people are tall and sleek. You don't see goiters or toothless mouths or milk-white eyeballs. The old women in the market stalls are well turned out. The shoeshine boys are clean and kempt. Asunción has so few beggars that they're known by name. There are slums. One of the worst is a squatter settlement on the mud flats below the cathedral. But the hovels have small yards and flowers and trees, and there's a clipped and chalk-lined soccer field in the midst of them. The cars on the streets are mostly old, but they're interesting old cars, like my airport taxi, the kind you used to see in American college towns – Volkswagen Beetles with Baja Bug front ends, comical 2CV Citroens, out-of-tune 914 Porsches with Bondo on the fenders and plumply dignified little Mercedes sedans from the 1950s. I was told that a lot of these cars were stolen in Brazil. If so, it's a tasteful and understated kind of car theft.

Another of Paraguay's happy surprises was seeing the US State Department going about its business there without a foot in its mouth or a thumb up its butt. This is because Paraguay is not a vital nation. Therefore the State Department is allowed to send a first-rate ambassador to Paraguay. Vital nations get political-appointment-type ambassadors – Arizona condominium developers who think the earth is flat but who are uniquely qualified to be ambassadors to vital nations because of the statesmanlike wisdom they exhibited in donating a jillion dollars to the Willie Horton Appreciation Day PAC in 1988. Actually, this is about what most vital nations – such as France, Israel and Japan – deserve. Anyway, the American ambassador to Paraguay, Timothy Towell, is not that type. He is educated, amusing, well-mannered and a career diplomat who even – and I'll bet this shocked the natives – savvies the lingo.

Ambassador Towell invited the American press to the embassy residence for a briefing and little sandwiches with the crusts cut off. Timothy Towell is a fine human, and the invitation proved his beautiful wife, Dane Towell, is another. Imagine having journalists in your own home and not even covering the furniture with plastic sheets first.

I'm afraid we weren't exactly the media's A team, either. None of us had the kind of wit, vision and heartfelt empathy for the underdog which characterizes, for instance, a Jane Pauley. The more important journalists were off reporting on more important elections, in Panama, Argentina, Bolivia and other countries that Americans know the whereabouts of or, anyway, get their dope from. We in the Asunción press corps called Paraguay 'The Land That Time Forgot – also *Life* and *Newsweek*'.

And this was one more nice thing about Paraguay, no important journalists. The clatter of rented helicopters, the yammer of electronic up-links, the hiss of inflating egos – it's impossible to get a decent siesta when important journalists are around.

I'm a particularly *un*important journalist. I can't even remember the 'Four Ws' or whether four is the number of Ws there are supposed to be. Which? Whatchamajigger? Whoa? What the fuck? It's something like that. So I was confused by the embassy briefing. Ambassador Towell kept going on and off the record. That is, sometimes when he said something he was 'Ambassador Towell'. And sometimes when he said something he was 'a highly placed diplomatic source'. True, it does make you feel mature and privileged to be spoken to off the record, like when you were a kid and your dad took you into a bar with him and on the way home he said, 'I don't think your mother has to know about this.' On the other hand it's a big responsibility trying to make sure the attractive and hospitable Towells don't wind up in the US embassy on the Ross Ice Shelf. Thus it was Ambassador Towell who said, 'I genuinely like this country,' and a highly placed diplomatic source who called it 'the former Tibet of South America'.

The gist of the briefing was that the coup had been fun. Paraguay's Presidential Palace, its Defense Department and the home of Stroessner's mistress (where the old goat was finally run to ground) are all within a few blocks of the American embassy. The diplomats got to stay up all night and use the embassy's emergency bunker and all its communications bells and whistles while mortar shells flew overhead. Maybe this doesn't sound like entertainment to you, but you have to understand that Asunción is a dull place.

'When Rodríguez came to power we assumed we were just getting a new general for an old one,' said a highly placed diplomatic source. 'Then Rodríguez did things that he said he was going to do.' The ambassador shrugged. His staff shrugged. The members of the press all shrugged.

Rodríguez has canceled the country's perennial state of emergency, eliminated censorship, legalized opposition parties, released political prisoners and welcomed exiled dissidents home. He has ordered prison torture cells destroyed, begun dismantling state economic controls and even launched a couple of corruption investigations (though not of himself). It's part of a worldwide trend in unaccountable and irrational dictator behavior.

Gorbachev, Jaruzelski, Roh Tae Woo, Pinochet – they're all acting nutty, and there have been outbreaks of freedom and democracy in such unlikely places as Estonia, Namibia, Hungary and the New York City mayoral race. Did somebody dip the International Monetary Fund debt notices in XTC? Don't tell me the CIA has finally done its job and infiltrated all these governments and is making them be good. 'Are diplomats supposed to be optimistic or cynical?' asked a highly placed diplomatic source.

That night I went out to a *parrillada*, a commercial version of that exotic Paraguayan custom known as a backyard cookout. I had a big piece of steak and a big glass of whiskey and more steak and more whiskey and a salad made out of a quarter head of iceberg lettuce – my kind of cuisine. Then I had an excellent cup of coffee, a cognac about the same vintage as that DC-8 and a big, smelly Cuban cigar. All told, it cost me eight dollars.

I walked back to the hotel with an American who'd been coming to Paraguay for a decade. At ten p.m. the downtown streets were mostly dark and wholly deserted. 'Don't worry,' said the American, 'it's safe to walk around at night. There's virtually no street crime. It has to be one of the last really safe places left in the world.' He paused as an ugly thought crossed his mind. 'I wonder if that will survive democracy, huh?'

There were some things about Paraguay which *did* make ugly thoughts cross your mind: a Nazi helmet for sale in a downtown antique store, ominously large embassies from naughty nations such as South Africa and Nationalist China, reports in the newly legal opposition press of 'secret graves' where Stroessner opponents were said to be numerous and a sign in Spanish advertising 'Von Stroheim's Tae Kwan Do Parlor' – the last an apparent effort to bring together a little bit of the worst in all the world's cultures. Also, for a country with only four and a half million people, a country that's been out of the Realpolitik loop for more than three centuries, Paraguay has a lot of war memorials, way too many.

Paraguay is a pleasant place all right, but not for the right reasons. It's not like the United States. It wasn't hard work, good luck and vigorous immigrant stock that made Paraguay nice. Paraguayan *tranquilo* is the product of a horrible and ridiculous history.

The conquistadors ignored Paraguay. It didn't have any gold. Wealth was to be gotten in farming, but the colonial Spanish were rarely tempted by manual labor. Madrid let missionaries do whatever they wanted with the place. In 1609 the Jesuits began gathering up the nomadic Indians, the Guaraní, and putting them into *reductions*. These were theocratic agricultural communes of about three thousand people where the Indians could be drilled in the use of Christian sacraments and the moldboard plow. Eventually some hundred thousand Guaranís were 'reduced'. The Spanish Jesuits, who wanted the Indians' souls for God, were quite brave about fighting off the Brazilian *banderiantes* who wanted the Indians' bodies for slavery. For this reason, and because the Jesuits didn't kill Guaranís or rape their women very often, the *reductions* of Paraguay became famous examples of utopia and the subject of a Robert de Niro movie, *The Mission*. Voltaire, Jesuit-hater though he was, called the *reductions* 'the triumph of humanity, expiating the cruelties of the first conquerors' and set part of *Candide* in Paraguay. Robert Southey, one of England's less talented poet laureates, wrote an immense poem about this alleged paradise:

> For in history's mournful map, the eye
> On Paraguay, as on a sunny spot,
> May rest complacent: to humanity,
> There, and there only, hath a peaceful lot
> Been granted, by Ambition troubled not . . .
> Etc., etc., etc., etc.

The *reductions* preserved Guaraní culture. Today ninety per cent of Paraguayans speak the Guaraní language. But at what cost, nobody ever bothered to ask the Guaranís. Perhaps the *reductions* were as pleasant as the collective farms we've seen in this century in the Ukraine and China. Anyway, when the Jesuits were kicked out of the New World in 1766, the Guaranís skedaddled and the *reductions* collapsed. This is generally called a tragedy in Paraguayan history, but it's hard to say where tragedies leave off and benefits begin in Paraguay.

The nation achieved independence in 1811 without firing a shot at the Spanish. There's some doubt if Spain even noticed. Paraguay was promptly taken over by a lunatic (and national hero) named Dr José Gaspar Rodriguez Francia. Dr Francia – elected *El Supremo* for life in 1814 – forced the Spanish upper class to intermarry with the *mestizos*. He forbade newspapers, fiestas and foreign trade. The clergy was suppressed. No one was allowed to emigrate. Immigrants were arrested and put to forced labor. Francia leveled Asunción and laid new avenues in a formal grid for fear conspirators might lurk in twisty back streets. He dressed all in black except for a scarlet cape and was fanatically honest with the national treasury – possibly the reason he was never known to smile. *El Supremo* died in 1840. More than a quarter century of his loathsome rule left Paraguay culturally homogeneous, economically self-sufficient, well-defended and possessed of a large budget surplus.

The next leader, Carlos Antonio López, freed political prisoners, granted citizenship to Indians, encouraged education and foreign investment, built one of South America's first railroads and is not nearly as well thought of today as Dr Francia.

Carlos López's son, Marshal Francisco Solano López, was another hero. *El Mariscal* is revered for destroying the nation. He was trying to play Argentina off against its traditional rival, Brazil, and he somehow managed to get into a war with Brazil and Argentina both and Uruguay besides. The War of the Triple Alliance lasted from 1865 to 1870. When it was done there was hardly a Paraguay left. Fifty-five thousand square miles had been conquered and annexed and the rest of the country was occupied, razed, starved, burned and pillaged. More than half the population was dead, including *El Mariscal* and eighty per cent of the adult males. To this day one of the nicest things about Paraguay is that there's no overcrowding.

Paraguayans are very proud of the War of the Triple Alliance. 'We fought desperately because we loved our land insanely,' as one war veteran too aptly put it.

It took Paraguay more than sixty years to recover. As soon as it did, it got into another amazingly bloody conflict you've never heard of – the Chaco War. This was fought with Bolivia from 1932 through 1935. One hundred thousand soldiers were killed battling over non-existent oil deposits in the Chaco, an immense region of grassland and thornbush populated mostly by dead soldiers.

Paraguay spent the following nineteen years recovering again while having ten presidents and the odd civil war and helping make Latin America the world's governance laughingstock. Then Stroessner arrived, bringing tyranny with shelf life; and for thirty-five years Paraguay had *tranquilo* (unless, of course, you were some kind of Commie or agrarian reformer or civil libertarian big-mouth, in which case you became permanently tranquil).

I was getting pretty tranquil myself. Paraguay was making me so mellow and content that I could feel my social conscience dribbling out my ears and IQ points flaking off my head like dandruff. Before long I had the brain of a tourist. I even caught myself getting interested in church architecture.

Paraguayan church architecture is no-nonsense stuff. The churches look like horse barns with verandas. But, inside, they're real retina-thrashers. The eighteenth-century church in the town of Yaguarón contains two thousand square feet of crazed whittling, a masterpiece of Paraguayan baroque. It's as ridiculously detailed as anything from the Europe of that era but with fun Guaraní Indian touches such as drug-trip color combinations and altar chairs with armrests that turn into snakes. I took a close look at some of the carved portraits of saints, and I think the Guaranís were pulling the padres' legs vis-à-vis conversion to Christianity.

Nearby in the town of Capiatá a modern woodcarver had created a one-man museum of Guaraní mythology. The front rooms of a large Spanish colonial house were filled with life-sized, that is, living-dead-sized Guaraní bugaboos such as the Plata Yryguy, a headless dog; the Corupi, a smug, plump fellow with his penis wrapped three times around his waist; the Kaaguy Pori, which has a big tentacle for a body, another tentacle for a leg, a bunch of tentacles for arms and tentacles growing out of its nose; and the Ao-Ao, which is too terrible to discuss. How convenient for the Guaranís that they had a mythology all ready to describe the conquering Spaniards and the subsequent history of Paraguay.

Paraguay is the size of California, so I didn't tourize it all. But I put five hundred miles on the rental car and was unable to find an ugly place except the Asunción Zoo. It was a very casual and dirty zoo where most of the cages were made of chain-link fence and fastened closed with twisted bits of wire. The hippo was chewing determinedly on its chain links and seemed three-quarters of the way to an escape. I don't know much about hippos. Are they one of those animals, like alligators, that look slow but *Wild Kingdom* always tell us can run faster than a horse? A lot of other cages had birds in them. There were cages full of chickens, ducks and pigeons as though the zookeepers just caged up whatever was handy. The bear cage smelled disgusting, and the bear looked dead. The puma cage smelled worse. The female puma was sleeping something off and the male puma was trying to get romantic but didn't seem to know what part of him he was supposed to stick in what part of her, romantically speaking. One small cage in a corner had a large ugly bird in it labeled 'Yryvu' with a small placard underneath reading '*Alimentación: animales putrefactos*'. And how.

If it weren't for *tranquilo* I could probably tell you what the

Asunción Zoo says about Paraguayan society and the Paraguayan political system. But, as it was, it was just a dirty zoo.

In truth, I can't even tell you what *Paraguay* says about Paraguayan society and the Paraguayan political system. I was doing for journalism about what the puma was doing for his mate. I did look up Martin Bormann in the phone book, but I guess he had an unlisted phone number. These Nazi war criminals are getting so old anyway, what would you do with them? Shorten one leg on their walker? Put a frog in their colostomy bag? Stick a playing card in their wheelchair spokes so they make a lot of noise and are easier for the Mossad to find?

I did finally go to a campaign event, in spite of myself. I got stuck in traffic in front of one.

A speech was being given by the principal opposition leader, Domingo Laino, presidential candidate of the Authentic Radical Liberal Party. This as opposed to the Fake Conventional Stingy Party, which, I guess, is what Rodríguez represents. Laino, a youthful-ish fifty-three, bewhiskered and just slightly thick around the middle, looked like a former college activist, which is what he is. Rodríguez supporters call him 'the detestable beard'. Stroessner used to throw him in jail a lot, so he can't be all bad. On the other hand, Stroessner never killed him, so maybe he's not *that* good.

Having covered the US presidential campaigns all through 1988, I was profoundly relieved to have absolutely no idea what the issues were in this election. The usual choice in Latin America is oppression combined with economically disastrous corruption causing a left-wing insurgency versus incompetence combined with economically disastrous social programs causing a right-wing coup. Laino has a Ph.D in economics, so he probably favors incompetence.

He's an impassioned and highly indignant orator, whatever his platform. The rally had begun at 2:00 p.m. I happened by at four and the Beard was still going strong. Whenever he said anything particularly indignant, the crowd would respond with the Jesse Jackson 'The People United/Will Never Be Defeated' chant. That was about all I could make out with my bar-floor Spanish. I stood below the podium trying to imagine what was being said with such vigor.

MY OPPONENT WEARS UNDERPANTS WITH LITTLE BUNNIES ON THEM!
HIS DAUGHTERS KISS BOYS THEY ARE NOT ENGAGED TO!
HE PUTS SINK WASHERS INTO THE POOR BOX AT CHRISTMAS AND HAS GIVEN INSULTING AND RIDICULOUS NAMES TO HIS DOGS!
VOTE FOR ME, I WILL TIE THE POINTS OF HIS SHIRT COLLAR TOGETHER UNDER HIS NOSE!
I WILL WIGGLE MY BEHIND AT HIS HOUSE!
I WILL GO ON THE RADIO AND SAY HIS NAME IN A MOCKING TONE OF VOICE!

This was a huge improvement on listening to political speeches and understanding them.

Well, fair's fair, so I went to a Rodríguez rally, too. Colorado is the real name of Rodríguez's party and the Colorados have functioned for the past forty-two years pretty much the way Italy's Fascist party used to. All public employees and military men are required to belong and dues are withheld from their paychecks. And there's an election law, cribbed from one written by Mussolini in 1923, that automatically gives a two-thirds congressional majority to the party that steals the most votes.

The Laino speech had been given in a public park and attracted five or six thousand people. They were a seemly, middle-class bunch who walked away at the end talking enthusiastically among themselves like tennis fans after a well-played match. 'What a prepositional phrase he has!' 'Those adjectives – incredibly precise!'

The Rodríguez stumper was more for the José six-pack crowd. It was held in the municipal soccer stadium with the police and the army cordoning off surrounding streets and scores of charter buses bringing in the party faithful. There were packs of food vendors and yards of banners and bushels of fireworks and two *polca* bands (not to be confused with polka bands, which are more melodious entirely). However, the turnout was not extra-ordinary, only about twice the Laino draw.

Rodríguez spoke from the top of the stands, where he was almost obscured by his overfed coterie. They looked like sausages in suits, cooking in the TV lights and about to split their polyester-blend skins. All I could see of the big man himself was a slice of plump forehead. Though, if a forehead can smile, his was doing it. Rodríguez has been all smiles ever since the coup.

The speech itself was a dull, pleasant thing. I kept hearing the words '*democracia*' and '*patria*' and '*necesario*'. I suppose Rodríguez was saying, 'Democracy is necessary for the country and the country is necessarily for democracy and with country and democracy together we can build the democracy that's necessary for the country,' with the soldiers and the police providing the unspoken subtext, 'Vote for me and goons won't come to your house and hit you in the head with a board.'

Whenever Rodríguez said anything particularly pleasant the stadium crowd would break into the same 'People United' chant that the Laino supporters used. Despite this evidence of double-barreled Jesse Jackson influence, no anti-Americanism was heard from either party. Maybe that's a testimony to Ambassador Tow-ell's diplomatic evenhandedness. Or maybe that shows how com-pletely out-of-it Paraguay really is.

The stadium infield was filled with the Colorado Party's most fervid supporters getting more fervid all the time on sugar-cane rum. They were operating noisemakers and compressed air sirens and were snake-dancing and waving huge Paraguayan flags, and sometimes they were just cutting loose and running in all directions like zanies. Hundreds of Colorado Party trademark red neckerchiefs made the scene look like a scout jamboree gone amuck.

I went out on the field and was quickly accosted by a group of Rodríguez supporters so fervid they could barely walk. Laino proponents had been thrilled by the sight of press credentials. Liberals have a quaint and touching faith that truth is on their side and an even quainter faith that journalists are on the side of truth. Not these stewed conservatives. There were five of them at the violently amiable stage of inebriation. They spoke a kind of collective English where one of them could pronounce a few words and a second understood a few words and a third explained to the first pair what they'd said and heard. A fourth began a performance in mime concerning the depth of his devotion to the pudgy general, falling at last to his knees and praying in the direction of Avoirdupois André. The five of them pushed me around for a bit, reading my credentials aloud and saying 'Rolling Stone', that is, 'Roy-ee-guh Stow-nay' over and over. After which the prayerful fellow insisted I write down his official title in some sublocal Colorado Party organization. (It is the beauty of well-designed fascism that it gives every piss-ant an ant hill to piss from.) Then the fifth and largest and homeliest of the group grabbed my notebook and pen and scribbled laboriously for ten minutes. I had this screed translated later and it turned out to be something that could have come from the opposition press editorial pages. It was a demand for 'absolute democracy' and for an end to mandatory party membership and for academic and religious freedom. And it came complete with my bully's signature and his government-identity-card number.

The prayerful guy took off his red neckerchief and shook it in my face. 'Colorado – no comunista! Colorado – no comunista!' he yelled, meaning that he wore red not because he was a Communist but because he was a member of the Colorado party. (Colorado, of course, means 'red' in Spanish, not 'overpriced ski resorts and dingbats who live in Boulder and teach feminist dance therapy'.) The five of them helped one another tie the material around my head Rambo-style, except most of it wound up hanging down in front of my face so I couldn't see anything. Then they all pumped my hand and shouted adiós.

Not everybody at the Colorado rally was quite this enthusiastic. I noticed later, in the stadium men's room, that somebody had used a red neckerchief to wipe his ass.

*

I spent election day itself in a little town called Tobatí, fifty miles east of Asunción. This was the first even slightly honest election in the history of Paraguay, and there was some confusion about the mechanics of voting. No one under the age of sixty had ever voted for anyone but Stroessner. I watched a peasant girl arrive at one of the polling places. She was checked off on the voter registration list and had her index finger dipped in ink so she couldn't vote again until she'd washed really well. She went into the *puerta obscura*, as the Paraguayans quite appropriately call a voting booth, came back out and asked the election officials something – who to vote for, I think. They made a little speech about *democracia*. The peasant girl went inside again and returned with a Colorado ballot and a quizzical expression, 'would this be good?' The election officials waved their arms and turned their heads away. This was supposed to be a *secret* ballot. One of the officials covered his eyes and held up an envelope. The girl came out of the booth the third time with envelope and ballot folded and refolded like a love note passed in a high-school class. She and the officials together couldn't get this wad through the slot in the ballot-box lid.

Rodríguez won the election, by the way.

I guess it's like love and marriage, political freedom being so poetic and noble when people are trying to achieve it and so boring and silly in practice. Well, something poetic and noble – and thoroughly awful – will happen soon in Paraguay if the past is anything to go by. In the meanwhile – *tranquilo*.

	RETURN
Nicaragua,	**OF THE**
	DEATH OF
February, 1990	**COMMUNISM**

On the morning of the twenty-sixth, the day after Violeta Chamorro's victory over Danny Ortega, I walked into the Inter-Continental hotel in Managua and Bianca Jagger was sitting alone in the lobby. Bianca had been ubiquitous during the election campaign: there was Bianca looking smart in an unconstructed linen jacket and yellow socks to match, Bianca looking serious with press pass and camera, Bianca looking thoughtful listening to Jimmy Carter, Bianca looking concerned conferring with Senator Christopher Dodd, Bianca looking committed in simple tennis shoes and neatly mussed hair, Bianca looking important wearing sunglasses after dark. But this morning Bianca looked . . . her age. Here we had a not very bright, fortyish, discarded rock-star wife, trapped in the lonely hell of the formerly cute – one bummed-out show-biz lefty.

I was feeling great myself, ready to turn somersaults over the Ortega defeat, full of good cheer and pleased with all the world. But then the forlorn, sagging little shape of Bianca caught my eye and, all of a sudden, I felt EVEN BETTER.

I hadn't come to Nicaragua prepared for such joy. Like most readers of papers and watchers of newscasts, I thought the Sandinistas were supposed to win this one. I'm a member of the working press; you'd think I'd know better than to listen to journalists. But there's a little bit of the pigeon in every good confidence man. I even believed the 21 February ABC-*Washington Post* poll that had Ortega leading Chamorro by sixteen percentage points. That is – I blush to admit this – I accepted the results of an opinion poll taken in a country where it was illegal to hold certain opinions. You can imagine the poll-taking process: 'Hello, Mr Peasant, I'm an inquisitive and frightening stranger. God knows who I work for. Would you care to ostensibly support the dictatorship which controls every facet of your existence, or shall we put you down as in favor of the UNO opposition and just tear up your ration card here and now?'

Furthermore, when I arrived in Nicaragua I found an Ortega political machine that was positively Bushian in its relentless drumming on the issue-free upbeat. Danny's smiling (I presume they used a photo retoucher) face and Danny's heartthrob-of-the-poli-sci-department moustache were everywhere to be seen. As was Danny – pestering babies, attempting dance steps, wearing Ed Begley, Jr, the-dog-was-sick-on-the-carpet shirts and tossing free baseballs into crowds of squealing totalitarianism fans. The Sandinistas' black and red, Doberman-mouth party colors were painted anyplace paint could stick. Sandinista songs played from every radio. The Danny for President slogan *todo sera mejor* (meaning 'everything will be better' and not, as I momentarily thought, 'major dried toads') was as perfect an all-purpose campaign promise as I have ever heard. There were Sandinista music videos with singing and dancing that could send Paula Abdul back to wagging pom-poms for the LA Lakers. And there were Sandinista ad campaigns tailored to every segment of the electorate. A billboard for city youth (the voting age is sixteen in Nicaragua) showed a moonstruck couple in Ortega T-shirts walking hand-in-hand toward a voting booth beneath the headline 'When you do it for the first time, do it for love.' Banners for the countryside showed a fierce portrait of Ortega with the motto *Daniel Es Mi Gallo*, 'Daniel Is My Fighting Cock'. (These can now be profitably recycled by the Kentucky Fried Chicken franchise outlets soon to open in Nicaragua.)

I confess I believed the Sandys had all the corners nailed down, and I spent the last couple of days before the election committing that original sin of journalism, 'writing the lead on the way to the ballpark'. What was I going to say about a loathsome Sandinista victory? I supposed I'd have to natter on about the unfair advantages of using state resources for party ends, about how Sandinista control of the transit system prevented UNO supporters from attending rallies, how Sandinista domination of the army forced soldiers to vote for Ortega and how Sandinista bureaucracy kept $3.3 million of US campaign aid from getting to UNO while Danny spent three million donated by overseas pinks and millions and millions more from the Nicaraguan treasury, etc.

But this seemed like weak-tea, crybaby stuff. No, I thought, I'll have to go shoveling in the manure pile of political science, trying to uncover the appeal that Marxism and other infantile world views still hold for people. One nice thing about being a conservative, at least I wouldn't feel betrayed by the masses. Democracy is only one of human liberty's safeguards and not always the most effective one. Back in the US we've got a House of Representatives full of bed-wetting liberals to prove it.

THE DOG IS DEAD BUT THE TAIL STILL WAGS.

That was what I planned to call this piece. (It's still a good title – I'll save it for my review of Christopher Hitchens' next book.)

Thus I was in a grim frame of mind when I went to the press conference held by that most ex- of America's ex-presidents, Jimmy Carter. The press conference was at the Sandinista's imposing media complex, one of the few buildings in Managua that won't fall down if you piss against the side of it. This propaganda palace was built with money donated by patsy Swedes, named after their bumped-off prime minister, Olof Palme, and hence called, by the small contingent of conservatives present, the 'Good Socialist Press Center'.

Carter was the head of one of the three principal international election-monitoring groups which were fluttering around Nicaragua pronouncing everything they saw fair and equitable. There was the United Nations ('the turkeys'), the Organization of American States ('the chickens') and Carter's group, the Council of Freely Elected Heads of Government ('the geese').

What Carter thought he was doing, besides proving there are worse things than Marines that the US can send to Nicaragua, I don't know. But there he was, the man who gave the store away in the first place, still grinning like a raccoon eating fish guts out of a wire brush and still talking in that prissy, nose-first, goober-grabber accent, except this time in Spanish: ' . . . new-WAY-vuh Knicker-RAH-wuh deh-muh-crat-TICK-uh . . . '

Carter oozed moral equivalence. 'There have been serious problems in the campaign process on both sides,' said Carter. 'We have to give credit to the Nicaraguan people for establishing an excellent electoral process,' said Carter. 'If the election is certified as honest and fair, the United States should lift sanctions,' said Carter. It's a shame Jimmy was too young to be an international observer at Germany's elections in 1932. 'We have to give credit to the German people for establishing an excellent electoral process.' Maybe he could have given Hitler some help rearming.

The 'press' at the press conference was a dirty and confused bunch, even by press corps standards. Inspection of credentials showed most of them to be correspondents for the Xeroxed news-letter of the Berkeley High-Colonic Liberation Front or television reporters from the Ann Arbor Reincarnation for Peace Coalition's public-access cable program. When a genuine newsman asked Carter about a report of UNO poll-watchers being arrested, the backpack journalists hissed.

A number of celebrity fellow travelers were in Nicaragua for the vote-off – Jackson Browne, Jimmy Cliff, the Sandinistas' Washington lawyer Paul (where's-the-Smith-Act-when-we-need-it) Reichler and Ed Asner, who didn't look like he'd missed any meals due to the injustice of the capitalist economic system. But the real show was the *sandalistas*, prosperous, educated lefties from the United States who've flocked to Nicaragua for a decade

33

to . . . well, to *help*. Although it's something of a puzzle why rebellious middle-class Americans went to Nicaragua to help San-dinistas wreck Central America, instead of, say, going to South Africa to help Boers chase schoolchildren with whips, or to Uganda to help Idi Amin eat people.

Some say the *sandalistas* are just young and dumb. But those folks are only half right. At first glance the Birkenstock Bolshies seem young. They wear 'youth' clothes and have adolescent body language – constantly distributing hugs and touches and squirming with emotion rather than sitting still in thought. But, looking closely at the uniform ponytails and earrings (many of the women wear them too), I noticed the tresses that were still long in back were oft-times gone on top, and the lady *sandalistas*, their underarm hair was streaked with gray.

A number of college-age kids were present, too – earnest and homely and not at all the type who would have been lefties in my day of high-fashion revolt. In 1968 these kids would have been in the ham radio club or Future Stenographers of America.

The Ortega-snugglers were dressed as though they were going to a Weather Underground Days of Rage costume party. They were all in jean skirts and drawstring pants, clogs, folk-art jewelry and tie-dyed tank tops – fashions fully twenty years out of style. I wonder what my hip friends and I in the summer of love would have thought about people wearing zoot suit jackets and reat pleat pants with key chains dangling to the ground.

The Carter press conference was on Saturday morning, the day before the election. That afternoon I attended a less complacent press conference given by the Center for Democracy at the Inter-Continental Hotel. The same bunch of backpack journalists were here, too, hissing even before anybody asked a question. Some of these life-style leftovers had gone so far as to don the red and black Sandinista neckerchief, which, like the neckerchief of Paraguay's fascist Colorado Party, is an item of apparel identical to that worn by the Boy Scouts of America. In Nicaragua the effect was of a scout troop gone deeply, seriously wrong, growing older and older but never graduating to Explorer and earning merit badges in 'Lenin', 'marijuana' and 'poor hygiene'.

I hadn't been keeping up to speed on Nicaraguan nonsense and had no idea why the lefties were heckling the Center for Democracy. The Center is one of those painstakingly bipartisan, painfully fair organizations that I usually heckle myself. CFD was the first election-monitoring group invited to Nicaragua. It was invited by both sides and had been observing the election campaign since the spring of last year. But now the CFD's credentials were downgraded so that its observers couldn't enter polling places, and more than fifty CFD observers had been denied Nicaraguan visas at the last minute.

The trouble was, the Center for Democracy had gotten caught telling the truth. CFD observers were at a UNO rally in the town of Masatepe on 10 December 1989, and they saw a Sandinista mob set upon Chamorro supporters with machetes. The mob killed one person and chopped the arms off a couple of others while the Sandinista police stood around like potted palms. Now, it's all right for observer groups to observe such things, that's what they're there for. But if the Sandinistas had wanted truth-telling groups, that's what they would have asked for. The OAS observers at the Masatepe rally obligingly waffled and claimed 'both sides' were to blame. But the CFD delegation – which included such dyed-in-the-hair-shirt liberals as Bob Beckel – was outraged by the Sandinista attack and said so.

Thus the press conference questions directed to Center for Democracy president Allen Weinstein weren't questions at all but diatribes capped with little rhetorical inquisitions such as, 'How are you going to overcome your bias?' and, 'Don't you think it's idiosyncratic that yours is the only observer group complaining about credential problems?' after which half the press conference attendees would clap. One particularly impassioned and bearded fellow named Carlos, a professor at Glendale College in California, where he teaches 'Chicano Studies', explained how the fact that the CFD was an observer group in the first place and came to Nicaragua at all proved its members had no respect for Nicaraguan sovereignty.

*

I'd gone to Nicaragua with the head of the National Forum Foundation, Jim Denton. Forum has been sponsoring interns from newly de-communized Eastern Europe, bringing them to the United States so that they can see how democratic institutions work and can learn to avoid making terrible mistakes like electing Jimmy Carter. Denton took two of these interns, Slawek Gorecki from Poland and Martin Weiss from Czechoslovakia, to Managua. Jim and I thought the *sandalistas* were funny. Martin and Slawek did not. They were sickened and enraged that citizens of a free nation would go somewhere to promote dictatorship. Even more than disgusted, they were mystified. Trying to explain American lefties to Martin and Slawek was like – simile fails me – trying to explain American lefties to two reasonable and intelligent people who'd never seen any.

Martin and Slawek – and Jim and I too, for that matter – preferred meeting with Commandante Raphael Solis, President of the Sandinista National Assembly. Here was a comprehensible scum bag, somebody who was making a buck off the evil he espoused.

Solis was master of the world-weary idealist act – lots of rueful smiles and care-laden brow rubs. His manners were gracious and welcoming, his grin warm and genuine. He was the kind of Commie who'd never ship anyone to a concentration camp in a boxcar; he'd send them in a taxi.

Solis said he was confident of an Ortega victory and of a large majority in the new National Assembly. But was he? With the improved sensitivity and increased intelligence that hindsight brings, I detect some loyal-opposition bullpen warm-up from Solis. He claimed he was looking forward to national reconciliation and hoped the UNO parties would play a part in it. He dismissed the statement by Interior Minister (and head of the secret police) Tomas Borge that the Sandinistas were 'prepared to lose the election but not to lose power'.

'That is,' said Solis with the aplomb of a born politician, 'campaign rhetoric'. He touted a *'perestroika* atmosphere' in Nicaragua, predicted 'foreign-policy compromises' and, in response to needling from Slawek he said, 'As to the changes in Eastern

Europe, I haven't heard any criticism from the Sandinista leadership. We think these changes are positive, democratic.' And he went on to claim that Nicaragua would be making the same changes soon and, also, had made them already.

At sunrise on election morning we headed around Lake Managua and north into the mountains, visiting polling places in Sebaco and Matagalpa and little villages in between. Then we drove further north to Jinotega in what had been Contra territory. Everywhere we went it was the same: awful roads through beautiful scenery to lousy towns. The whole country is cracked, shattered, dirty, worn-out. Everything dates from the Somoza era or before. Ten years of revolution have produced nothing but the Olof Palme Press Center. Even the lamest People's Republic cosmetic touches were missing. Sandinista graffiti is the only fresh paint in Nicaragua. The nation looks – and smells – like that paradigm of socialism, a public restroom.

The voting was done in dingy schoolrooms with all the window glass broken or missing and bare wires running across the ceiling to fifteen-watt light bulbs. Every voter had the ballot-marking process explained to him personally so that the election went forward at the speed of mammal evolution. People were waiting in line by the hundreds to vote.

Each polling place was run by a brisk, snippy, managing Sandinista woman of middle age, the kind of woman who, in a free society, is known as 'my first wife'. Denton, Martin, Slawek and I didn't have the proper credentials to enter polling places, but we did anyway and, for the most part, got away with it – though at the price of being treated like ex-husbands.

The UN, the OAS and the Carter group were all going around doing about the same thing we were in the way of checking for vote fraud. That is, they popped their heads in and made sure there was no Sandinista with a pistol in a toddler's ear saying, 'Vote for Danny or the rug monkey gets it.' We didn't see any cheating like that, and the UN, the OAS and the Carter group said they didn't either.

We did see a truckload of soldiers being hauled around to vote. 'Who are you for?' we yelled. '*Cinco! Cinco!*' they shouted, holding up five fingers to indicate they were voting for the fifth line on the ballot, the Sandinistas. '*Uno*', said one little fellow in the back, and they all giggled and made as if to pummel him.

In the village of San Ramón we saw some horseplay. The men and women had decided to get in separate lines. Then the line of men shoved the line of women off the school porch and into the rain. The women confided to us that the men were going to vote for Ortega.

And we saw former Democratic presidential hopeful Bruce Babbitt standing around at one polling place, looking clueless. Jim Denton said, 'That's Bruce Babbitt,' but for the life of me I couldn't remember who Bruce Babbitt was. I guess this tells us all we need to know about Bruce's political future.

The only Nicaraguan we heard complain was a guy who wasn't allowed to vote because he was drunk. 'He admits that he's drunk,' the Sandinista policeman told us. 'Everybody makes mistakes,' the drunk told us. And we told the policeman, 'They let Teddy Kennedy vote in the Senate.'

When we came back through Sebaco late in the afternoon, some of the same people who'd been standing in line to vote at seven that morning were still waiting. 'We've been in line since four in the morning, since three in the morning, since two in the morning,' one person told us with cheerful rural vagueness about time. 'And if it is necessary we will stay here until . . . *ten!*' said another man, naming the latest hour of the evening he could think of offhand.

Of course people don't stand in line for twelve hours in drizzly weather at the ass end of nowhere to vote for the status quo. So there were three hints I'd been given that Ortega might lose. But there's no getting through to the highly perceptive. It wasn't until another journalist told me the Sandinistas were in trouble that I believed it.

We'd gone back to the Olof Palme Center to wait for returns.

Around 11:00 p.m. a network television newsman with (don't be shocked) left-wing connections came by looking agitated. 'P.J., I was just over at Sandy headquarters and something's gone seriously wrong,' he said, meaning the opposite. 'All of Ortega's people are really upset. The early returns show them getting . . .' Getting what the billboard said when you do for the first time, you should do for love.

The UNO people had heard the same buzz and were in a mood of contained but swollen hope. Chamorro's coalition was holding its election-night party at a restaurant in one of Managua's few remaining middle-class enclaves. The crowd was a model of bourgeois propriety. Occasionally someone would stand on a chair and say, *'Viva UNO'* in a loud voice, but that was about it. The place was all clean shirts, hearty handshakes, polite honorifics and, 'How's your brother in Miami?' It was difficult to picture these decent, hard-working, prosperous, common-sensical people overthrowing a government. Sometimes it's hard to remember that bourgeois propriety is the real revolutionary force these days. All over the world we're bringing down dictatorships – or at least forcing them to go condo.

The Sandinista 'victory party' was, on the other hand, a massive street disco populated by kids who in the US would have been selling crack, getting the name of their favorite heavy metal band tattooed on their butts or planning a drive-by shooting. These are the last people on earth that *sandalista* types would consort with back home. But all sorts of big, homely dirty-haired American girls in stained T-shirts and dweeby little chicken-necked American boys in ripped jeans were fraternizing the hell out of the lumpen Nicaraguans (who were dressed in their Sunday best, by the way).

There was no evidence of Danny difficulties at the street dance, really no trace of politics except the general air of thuggishness that hangs over all 'mass' political movements. Lots of beer and cane liquor was being consumed and much smooching in the shadows was being done and fistfights and lunch-blowings were beginning to dot the crowd. After half an hour of walking around with our hands over our wallet pockets, we decided our little group of *wing-tipistas* belonged back at the Chamorro party or – even better by the standards of the bourgeois propriety revolution now afoot – asleep in our beds.

I awoke to the sound of lugubrious Spanish on the television. It was Danny Boy giving his concession speech, old Landslide Daniel. I understand Jimmy Carter had tracked Danny down in the middle of the night and told him – loser-to-loser – the jig was up. The Sandinistas had done everything they could to ensure the validity of this election in the eyes of the world. Now they had to eat what they had cooked. Quite a bit of 'crow in red sauce' was served around the globe in 1989 and '90.

Danny's speech was a long one. There are no brief excuses for communism. And it was punctuated with more pauses for dramatic effect than a high school production of *Macbeth*. Lined up behind Daniel was most of the Sandinista *nomenklatura*, pouting and sniffling and generally looking like dear Uncle Bill had died and left his fortune to the cat. At the end of Danny's speech, he and his pals raised their fists in the air and warbled the Sandinista battle anthem, the one with the last line about Yankees being 'the enemies of all humankind', singing us farewell in the manner of the Mickey Mouse Club, except this crowd couldn't carry a tune on a shovel. The TV cameras pulled back to show the Olof Palme press corps singing along through their tears.

Me, I was singing myself, making up little tunes and dancing and capering around:

> Benjamin Linder was blown to a flinder,
> Dennis Wilson run o'er by a train,
> Now it's hasta luego to Danny Ortega,
> And United Fruit's come back again!

I rushed out to gloat. I especially wanted to gloat over the Americans – the ripe-suck liberals and MasterCard Marxists – see them backing and filling and blowing smoke out their pants cuffs. At the Inter-Continental, across the lobby from Bianca, Paul Reichler was excusing the Nicaraguan people to the news media, saying they had 'voted with their stomach'. The poor misguided fools. I suppose they should have voted with their ____hole, Paul Reichler. A few yards away that human rum-blossom Senator Chris Dodd was telling reporters the election 'wasn't a victory for UNO. The Nicaraguan people just wanted change.' Yes, yes. And the 1988 presidential race wasn't a victory for Republicans either. The American people just wanted Michael Dukakis ground into a heap and sold as fiber supplement.

Driving through the streets of Managua, seeing American hippy-dips all fiddle-faced and dejected, it was hard to resist the temptation to yell things out the car window. 'Get a job!' Or, 'What's the matter with your legs, toots, don't you know "Fur is dead"?' In fact I couldn't resist it. My favorite thing to do was just make a little pistol motion with my hand and shout, 'Nicolae Ceausescu!!!'

I headed for the Olof Palme Center to rank on the backpack journalists. Oh, it was almost too sweet for telling, how they bellyached and sourpussed and went around in sulks. Carlos, the professor of 'Chicano Studies', tried to look on the sunny side. 'We can't abandon the people of Nicaragua,' he said with a straight face, and, 'The struggle will continue. People will be even more committed.' But in the end, Carlos was reduced to racism in his attempt to explain why the polls said Danny would win but the voters said otherwise. 'It's the Latino culture,' said Carlos. 'People love to say one thing and do another.'

The younger *sandalistas* looked like they'd just seen Lee Atwater open for the Grateful Dead. They weren't angry, really, just deeply, deeply disappointed. Here they'd blown their semester break and Mom was going to have a cow when she got the VISA bill for the plane ticket, and then the Nicaraguan people went and let them down like this. But the old *sandalistas*, the New Left geezers, they looked like they'd gone to hell in a bong. It's into the trash can with this sixties litter, and you could see they knew it. They looked like Abbie Hoffman was looking the last couple of years of his life, as though every night when they go to sleep a BMW chases them through their dreams.

*

And in that BMW, or hoping to be there soon, were all the regular Nicaraguans down at the Eastern Market.

Were they surprised that UNO won? They laughed. 'We expected victory, especially the mothers,' said a mother.

'All the mothers are happy,' said another mom.

'We hope Violeta fulfills her promises,' said the proprietess of a shoe store. 'Or we'll get rid of her too,' she added in the tone of an experienced democrat.

'If Ortega doesn't give in, the people will rise up,' said a cobbler. 'We have *other countries* that will help us.' And he nodded toward the Congressional Press Gallery ID I was wearing around my neck.

'What about the polls?' I asked. 'Why were they so wrong?'

'People were afraid,' said a man in a barbershop.

'The same old experts who always come here came here and gave us the same old results they always give,' said the barber.

Another customer began yelling, 'All we had to eat was old lard and the kind of sugar they feed to cattle!'

And that set off a passing drunk who may have been confused about geopolitics – or maybe not – but, anyway, had the right attitude. 'Tomorrow, Japan!' he shouted.

RETURN OF THE DEATH OF COMMUNISM, PART III — THE SAGA CONTINUES

Kiev and Tibilisi,

September 1991

'Do they remember the good times? "Yes, under Stalin in the early 1950s. There was enough food and there was order." What do they want for their grandchildren? "Lots of food and order."'
—NATALYA KRAMINOVA, INTERVIEWING RUSSIAN VILLAGERS FOR THE MOSCOW NEWS, 22 SEPTEMBER 1991

Kiev

It's impossible to get decent Chinese takeout in China, Cuban cigars are rationed in Cuba, and that's all you need to know about communism. But communism illegal in the USSR or the Soviet Union or the Union of Sovereign So-and-So Republics or whatever they're calling themselves, when you order Chicken Kiev in Kiev . . . 'Chicken is finish,' said the large, mopey waiter, making two fists and banging his forearms together in the national signal for 'we're out of it or we're closed or anyway the hell with you.'

I never did get to place an order. 'Is beefsteak,' the waiter explained when he'd returned from the hour-long hourly break which is the customary right of all Soviet food-service employees.

43

A plate full of something and cabbage was deposited in front me. It was, in fact, beef, though not the steak kind. It tasted right, but this was Monday. I would get 'beefsteak' for lunc every day that week. I would order veal, pork, fish and som thing I couldn't pronounce, and I would get beefsteak. Monday beef was, as I said, fine. Tuesday's was middling. Wednesday wasn't very good. Thursday's was pretty bad. And Friday's w the color of gunmetal and smelled. That was when I realize that all my beefsteaks had been cut from the same large an increasingly elderly piece of beef.

Marina, my Intourist guide, said this was the best restaura in Kiev. At the table next to mine another smaller, more da druffy waiter was chatting up a customer's date. The little wait filled her wineglass, managing to dribble some of the wine himself. Then he grabbed the skirt of the tablecloth and wip his hands. Over by the kitchen door the restaurant's busboy w drinking the dregs out of mineral-water bottles. In the kitch itself three or four people were conducting a loud quarrel punc ated with thrown pans. And a total of seven restaura employees were operating the cash register. They passed n lunch tab around among themselves for almost half an ho before I was allowed to pay the bill, which amounted to 16 ruble 53 cents.

But you couldn't blame communism. Communism w illegal. And communism was extra-specially double-illegal in Kie – Kiev being the free and democratic capital of the entirely an completely, you-bet independent republic of the Ukraine. On September, the day I arrived, there was a huge rally downtov where thousands of citizens cheered as members of the Ukrai Parliament officially declared the Ukraine independent. 'This the fourth time they have officially declared this,' said Marin So I guess independence in these parts works the same way tl restaurants do. Anyway, the Ukraine was independent, and tl only reason it didn't have borders and money and an army an a post office was that the people in charge of those things we waiting for somebody to add up their lunch checks.

You could tell for sure that there was no more communis

the Ukraine because all the giant statues of Communists had
en hit in the face with paint bombs. Every bronze, concrete
d marble Communist had a big white paint splash across the
sser, making the Ukraine look like a country that acquired
national heros in a custard-pie fight. In the main square a
rticularly huge statue of Lenin – which, besides paint-bomb
sfigurement, had KILLER and FASCIST graffitied on its base – was
ing torn down (or would have been if anyone could have found
e crane operator). All the avenues, plazas and thoroughfares
mmemorating Bolshevism were getting 'Oak Street'-type moni-
rs. And the most popular piece of wearing apparel was a stone-
ashed denim shirt with a label over the breast pocket reading
S Army'.

Private enterprise had appeared in Kiev, at least a larval stage
it. Street vendors didn't exactly hawk their wares but they did
behind tables and impassively offer for purchase books,
wers and clothes. Almost every neighborhood had a private
arket selling food – good food. There were big, fat potatoes in
ppertone skins; turnips the size of artillery shells; beets with
grand cru tint; noble, leonine heads of cabbage; pot cheese with
rds in folds as white as tuxedo shirts; and melons as big and
sh as diaper-commercial babies. The meat counters were
pressive, too, though not someplace you'd take k.d. lang on
date. Massive chunks of animals were being heaved around and
opped to pieces. Tongues, brains, hooves, feet and personal,
ivate parts decorated the cutting boards. The tile floor was
ppy with blood puddles. But the meat was good-looking if
u could bear to look: pink-champagne-colored pork, beef red
e valentines and crocheted with savory fat, good teeth in the
eep skulls and clear eyes staring from the future-soup-stock
w heads.

They were fabulous markets. They'd do any nation proud.
cept for one little problem – no customers. Some people were
andering around but it was the kind of wandering that Ameri-
ns do in Porsche showrooms. Prices in the private markets
ere high. Meat was selling for 25 rubles a kilo. That's 38 cents
pound, but the average Ukrainian makes 250 rubles a month.

So 38 cents a pound is like going to the Safeway and getting ounces of London broil for a hundred bucks. But it wasn't pove alone that made the private markets such dysfunctional a unbustling places. Prices weren't just high, they were bizarre. I one thing, they were all the same. Each babushkaed grandmot selling lentils was selling lentils for the same price as every oth grandmother – no premium for quality, no discount for quant and no haggling.

I asked Marina about the beef. I said, 'Isn't beef cheaper t time of year? I mean, if you don't slaughter cattle in the fall, th you have to feed them in the barn all winter, and, especially a country with a grain shortage, I'd expect lots of people wou be bringing cattle to market right now, increasing supply a driving down prices.'

'No,' said Marina.

'Now pigs, on the other hand,' I said, 'are raised on slo and people are going to be tossing out food scraps year 'rour so the price of pork would tend to remain constant.'

'Meat,' said Marina, 'sells for twenty-five rubles a kilo.'

'Beef and pork, they both sell for the same price?'

'Meat,' said Marina, 'sells for twenty-five rubles a kilo.'

'Fresh spring lamb?'

'Twenty-five rubles a kilo.'

'Stringy old mutton?'

'Twenty-five rubles a kilo. Meat,' said Marina, 'sells twenty-five rubles a kilo.'

There was another way to buy food in Kiev, at the state fo stores with their long, scuffling lines at the head of which w nothing, just about nothing at all. There was bread, sometim that you could use as a medicine ball or a boat anchor. The were ten or a dozen five-gallon jars full of murky liquid wit few unidentifiable pickled things resting in the bottoms and ot jars of the same kind which contained plain water. The sausag when there were any to see, were a shock and a horror, looki like nothing but discarded sex toys. The produce was appalli The potatoes resembled gray prunes and no other vegetable w distinguishable from compost.

But the prices were right. The state store's carrots – which would have passed as criminal evidence, wizened remains of a kidnap victim's severed fingers maybe – cost 50 kopecks. And a kopeck is three-thousandths of a penny. The carrots in the private markets cost six times as much. Thus the Soviet economy is undermined by a kind of reverse black market from an anti-matter universe, a black market where it is legal to buy things you don't want too cheaply.

Every aspect of material life in the Soviet Union works this way. If you stand in line long enough the state provides goods and services. The services are out of service and the goods are no good, but food, clothing, shelter and medical care are – just barely – available. And they are hilariously inexpensive. The babushkas in the private markets don't really have to sell you anything. They're there to make money, not a living. If you don't buy the food, well, then . . . fist/fist, forearm/forearm . . . they'll take it home and eat it themselves, and you can stand in line for mummified carrots.

Marina, eyeing a selection of lard in a broken dairy cooler at the state food store, said, 'The two most difficult things in the Soviet Union are getting enough food and losing weight.'

An American's first reaction to the Soviet Union is to roll up his sleeves. There is so much to be done. Of course, that's true in any poor country, but in the Soviet Union there is the what with which to do it. Give an American a couple of gallons of paint, some Murphy's oil soap, a mop and a can of Lysol spray disinfectant and the private food markets would look like Balducci's. The beefsteak restaurant could be fixed in an afternoon, just turn anybody's grandmother loose in there with a Fannie Farmer cookbook, a copy of *Emily Post's Etiquette* and a .38 revolver. Something could even be done with the lurching, squealing, backfiring, oil-dribbling Volga sedan in which I was being driven around town. Two cans of Bondo and it's a 1956 Studebaker President – a real collector's item on the classic-car market.

Not that the Soviets are incapable of helping themselves.

Marina described how her friends take local goods to Poland a sell them for hard currency (it says something that Soviets con sider the zloty a hard currency) then fly to Turkey because that the cheapest Western country (it says more that Soviets consid Turkey a Western country). In Turkey they buy clothes and d goods and bring these back and sell them for a sizable profit consignment stores. But Marina was embarrassed by this. 'W hate to be seen trading,' she said. 'It makes us feel almost lil Negroes.'

Out in the country north of Kiev the topsoil was turned u in lustrous brunet furrows and smelled so rich it seemed like yo wouldn't need to grow food, you could just cook soup from th loam itself (the beefsteak restaurant tried this). The peasa houses were big and well-proportioned, made of clay-tile bricl with hipped roofs of tin sheeting. Doors and windows we deep-set in elaborately carved wooden frames. On the secor story of most houses was a large glassed-in porch, the Ukrainia equivalent of a Florida room, a Siberia salon perhaps. The hom all had generous yards surrounded by Tom Sawyer board fence many with the palings painted alternately blue and yellow, th Ukrainian national colors. These quaint but substantial hom could be sold by the thousands as vacation getaways for tw income urban professional families if only the Ukraine could I made trendy. And who knows? Fashion is an odd thing. Colle tive farming may replace skiing or tennis as the thing to do Hollywood executives could start driving wheat combines work. And Ralph Lauren might bring out a Potato Digger line leisure clothes. This would be a great relief to the Ukrainia peasants, who would then be able to move somewhere – an where – besides these handsome villages surrounded by the be farm land in the world.

Because there was nothing in those villages. There were r stores except the state food stores and no food in these. Out the fields men and women were using the kind of wooden far implements which decorate walls in the United States. The were no roads, just mud spaces impassable for half the year. 'A least the highway to Kiev is well-paved,' I said to Marina. Sh laughed. The highway was paved because this was the highway to the dachas belonging to high officials in the Ukrainian Communist Party. (Not that they're high officials in the Ukrainian Communist Party anymore, now they're high officials in the National Government of the Ukraine.) The peasant's houses all had wells outside, with cranks and buckets and little roofs over them. I thought they were lawn ornaments. They were the only source of water. The wells were shallow and there were no sewers, only cesspits even shallower than the wells. If any of these had really been wishing wells, what the peasants would have wished for was clean water. And it was all so easily put right – one day with a drilling rig and a pick-up truck full of cheap pipe would do it. Even Soweto has indoor plumbing. A septic tank is nothing but a concrete box, and, to judge by Soviet architecture, the locals were plenty capable of making one. The Dnieper river was only a few miles away. A couple of cartloads of riverbed gravel, some shovel work and a tractor or an ox or the kids pulling a log drag would make for weatherproof roads.

'We need some economist to give us a plan,' said Marina.
'You had that already,' I said.

We drove about fifty miles north on the dacha highway to the edge of the 'closed zone' around Chernobyl. The zone has a radius of just eighteen miles. Right outside, food crops were still growing, dairy cows were still grazing and people were still living – sick, maybe, but still living. The irradiated ground did not glow or make drive-in-movie noises. No giant mutant predators or revivified lizard monsters stalked across it. I would have felt better if I'd seen one. A cicada the size of Space Mountain would have gotten somebody's attention, even in the Soviet Union. But radiation doesn't have very immediate or clearly visible effects, so nothing very immediate or clearly visible was being done about it. The border of the closed zone was one strand of barbed wire. There was a checkpoint on the road with a sign reading, 'Citizen, attention. You enter a place of special regime.' Another sign warned visitors not to hunt, fish, swim, camp, pick mushrooms or drink water.

Three atomic reactors (one of which has since caught fire) were still operating at Chernobyl. A busload of men and women coming home from work stopped on the other side of the checkpoint. None wore protective clothing. The bus was given a cursory check with a Geiger counter. The workers passed in one door of a little shed and out another faster than passengers go through an airport metal detector. They looked depressed, but, then again, everybody in the Soviet Union looked depressed.

'Do you want to interview them?' said Marina.

'I want to know why they're still working there.'

'For pay,' said Marina. And I couldn't think of anything else to ask.

On our way back we stopped to look at a hydroelectric dam with rusty sluice gates and unkempt high-tension wires. It was immediately upriver from the city. Thirty-three feet of water loomed above downtown Kiev – a Super-Soaker of Damocles held in place by the same quality of materials and engineering that went into the Chernobyl reactors.

Marina was pessimistic about the dam. 'One day – woosh.' Marina was pessimistic about everything. She explained how it was now legal for Soviet citizens to buy Western goods in the special hard-currency shops but still illegal for them to own hard currency. 'We visit these stores like you would visit a museum,' she said. (She meant Porsche dealership.) Nothing had happened with land reform. 'It's like knocking on a door that isn't there,' said Marina. And, although all the property of the Communist Party had been confiscated, it had been confiscated by the state that was created by this Party. 'So, what,' I said, 'does that mean?' Marina shrugged.

Marina's grandfather had been a government official in the Ukraine when Stalin was in power, and, like many government officials then, he'd been sent to a prison camp. He got out only because Stalin died. None the less, Marina grew up with a certain faith in the Soviet system. Then when she was in high school in the 1970s she heard Alexander Solzhenitsyn's *Gulag Archipelago* being read on Radio Liberty broadcasts from the West. 'This upset me terribly,' she said. In 1979 she was allowed, as an Intourist guide, to travel to Western Europe. She spent the first hard currency she ever possessed on Solzhenitsyn books, which she could only find in English. She hid them carefully in her luggage because she knew that if they were found, she wouldn't be traveling to Western Europe again.

Marina read these books aloud to her family. They sat every night around the kitchen table with Marina translating, a Russian–English dictionary by her side for words she didn't recognize. 'Too many intellectuals were killed, imprisoned,' said Marina. 'No one wants to be an intellectual here. In America you call somebody a fool, we call them an intellectual.'

Tibilisi

There was no shortage of foolish intellectuals in the Republic of Georgia. And they all had guns.

Georgia is, of course, claiming independence from the Soviet Union. The whole Soviet Union is claiming independence from the Soviet Union. And all the independent places have places claiming independence from them. Something called South Ossetia is trying to secede from Georgia. I'll bet South Ossetia starts having trouble with South-Central Ossetia soon. And what was once the second most powerful nation in the world is becoming a collection of countries with names like 'The Republic of Me and You and I'm Not Sure About Me'.

But that's not why the intellectuals had guns in Georgia. They weren't rebelling against somebody else's government. They were rebelling against their own.

Last May Georgia held its first free elections since the Neolithic Age and elected one Zvaid K. Gamsakhurdia president. Gamsakhurdia (pronounced sort of like 'Gram's accordion' but

51

not really) is a distinguished-looking, hammy-acting university professor and a prominent Georgian nationalist. He helped found the local Helsinki Watch civil-liberties monitoring group, was convicted by the Brezhnev government of monitoring civil liberties and was sent to jail for it. Gamsakhurdia was quite the local hero and was elected by an 87 per cent margin.

Once in office, however, Gamsakhurdia began acting like a butt-head. He closed newspapers, arrested opposition leaders, fired everybody in the government who didn't agree with him, spent $460,000 on bullet-proof Mercedes limousines, forbade Georgians to sell meat, vegetables or building materials anywhere except Georgia, blocked business privatization and land-reform programs and accused the United States of conspiring with Moscow to prevent Georgia from becoming independent.

So Georgians began to demonstrate. Thousands of them marched up and down Rustaveli Prospect, Tibilisi's main street. The anti-Gamsakhurdia protesters occupied their own opposition-party headquarters, but that seemed inadequate, somehow, so they took over the National Congress Building and swore to stay there until . . . I'm not sure until what. The government responded, not by attacking the protesters but by calling on protesters of its own to protest in favor of itself. Gamsakhurdia went on national television and asked people from all the little towns and villages of Georgia to come to the capital and protect him. And come they did, in scores of flag-decked buses. Thousands more Georgians marched up and down Rustaveli Prospect. Police used the village buses to build barricades around the National Government Building, down the street from the National Congress Building, and the pro-Gamsakhurdia protesters swore to stay there until whatever, too.

Actually, the government did attack the opposition a little bit. On 2 September, Georgian Special Security Forces (which may not have been very special because up until 2 September Georgia hadn't had any Special Security Forces) shot at some demonstrators. But, despite a lot of impassioned rhetoric, no one managed to die until 21 September, when a thirty-five-year-old cardiologist set himself on fire in front of the National Opera

Building, on Rustaveli between the National Congress Building and the National Government Building, leaving a note saying, 'If Georgia needs blood to settle the conflict then take mine.' Although, up until then, Georgia hadn't.

Meanwhile Georgia's National Guard – which is commanded by a sculptor and looks about as professional as a group of middle-aged duck hunters – split into two groups professing neutrality. One group was neutral and prepared to defend the nation against opposition lawlessness, and one group was neutral and prepared to defend the nation against government oppression.

The anti-Gamsakhurdia protesters and the part of the National Guard that was neutrally on their side then took over the national television station, but, since this is a very bureaucratic society, they stormed the offices of the television station's bureaucracy, leaving the government with the actual broadcast facilities.

If none of this makes sense it's because – believe me, I was there – none of this makes sense.

Georgia was less perfectly depressing than the Ukraine. The food was better. The weather was cute. The Caucasus Mountains are – I don't think I'm saying this just because I'm Caucasian – really beautiful. Tibilisi, the capital of Georgia, squats prettily in the Kura River valley about 160 miles inland from the Black Sea at what was once the extreme southeast corner of Hellenic civilization. Medea, of Golden Fleece fame, was from Georgia. After Medea got divorced by her Argonaut husband, Jason, she murdered Jason's second wife, tore her own sons limb from limb and ran off to Athens in a chariot pulled by dragons. I'm told that this, except for the dragons, is not untypical Georgian behavior. Stalin was from Georgia, too.

Anyway, Tibilisi is sort of charming and old. There are little, crimped streets overhung with New Orleans-style balconies, some Constantinople Jr churches, lots of midget stucco houses with grape vines tangling their patios and only a large – rather than an infinite – number of horrible communist cement apartment houses. The city has been destroyed forty times in Georgia's quarrelsome fifteen-hundred-year history, but not lately. In 1801 the last king of Georgia – named, as you might have guessed, George – turned the whole country over to Russia. If Stalin, Medea and the protesters on Rustaveli Prospect are anything to go by, who can blame him?

There were huge demonstrations the night I arrived. I wasn't scheduled to meet my Intourist guide until the next morning. I don't speak a word of Georgian and the only word of Russian I speak – *tovarish*, 'comrade' – is a word you don't say anymore. So I didn't have any idea who was demonstrating against what. I knew the opposition was made up of intellectual urban elites, and I knew the pro-government people were peasants and factory workers, but everybody dresses so badly in the Soviet Union that it was impossible to tell which was which. All of them, including some members of the National Guard, were wearing those stone-washed denim shirts with 'US Army' on the pocket.

Sometimes the two sides marched around ignoring each other and sometimes the two sides argued with each other and sometimes I couldn't tell for sure if there really were two sides. I gave up and went to my hotel, where I found the restaurant closed because – as best I understood – 'it was dinner time'.

This hotel was just off Rustaveli, around the corner from the occupied National Congress Building (though I didn't know that was what it was). I left the door to my balcony open so I could hear if whoever started fighting with whomever else. Which, at three in the morning, they did, but I slept through it.

When I woke up everybody was really mad. Barricades and sitters-in had been forcibly removed from the Congress Building. My Intourist guide, Nina, and I drove to the TV station, where Nina went looking for people for me to interview. She produced a large, bearded fellow still blood-splattered from being whacked on the head early that morning. 'I will never move from here! I will defend democracy! I want the world to know!' he said, although what he wanted the world to know I had a hard time

54

getting him to tell me. Not that I understood when he finally did. According to my notes, pro-Gamsakhurdia protesters approached the barricades at the Congress Building in a friendly manner so that the bearded man thought they were coming for a reconciliation. But then they attacked the barricades with a crane. Three a.m. seems an odd time to be reconciled and a crane an unlikely item to bring on the errand, but never mind. 'Stones were thrown.' The bearded man got hit by one 'the size of a cabbage'. Pro-Gamsakhurdia protesters further attacked him, pushing him into a building, but then, when these attackers saw that he was covered in blood, they helped him out of the building and tried to get him to an ambulance. However, he was attacked by other pro-Gamsakhurdia protesters, but the pro-Gamsakhurdia protesters who'd attacked him first attacked the attackers, drove them back and got him medical treatment after all. 'I really felt the support of those people who attacked us,' said the bearded man.

Several thousand people were gathered at the TV station, most of them infected with that happy sense of purpose people have when they are standing up for a principle they haven't really been knocked down for yet. People who direct mob scenes in movies have obviously never seen a mob. Movie mobs are decided and purposeful and achieve instant internal government by means of one guy who stands on a chair and yells, 'hanging's too good for 'em'. Then off the mob goes to lynch Sidney Poitier. Real mobs just mill around acting pointlessly upset while being addressed by a series of half-important people speaking into PA systems that turn all human speech into car-theft-alarm noises. Nobody knew what was going on, which made everybody talk loudly about what was happening, and it was embarrassing if you talked too loudly because then everyone in the mob would come cluster around you hoping to hear some bewilderment more illuminating than their own.

Nina took me to talk with the leaders of the TV-station protest. This was one of five or six political interviews that I did while I was in the Soviet Union – with Ukrainian Nationalists, Ukrainian non-Nationalists, a member of the Ukrainian Parliament, anti-Gamsakhurdian Georgians, pro-Gamsakhurdian Georgians and some people I don't know who they were.

I can tell you what they all had to say, if you like, I mean if you're having trouble getting to sleep or something. I would ask them what their group advocated, and they would say, 'Democracy must be defended.' I would ask, 'How do you propose to do this?' They would say, 'There must be a structure of democracy in our society.' I would ask, 'What are your specific proposals?' They would say, 'We must build democratic institutions.' I would ask, 'By what means?' They would say, 'Building democratic institutions is necessary so that there is a structure of democracy in our society at all levels.' And by this time I'd be yelling, 'BUT WHAT ARE YOU GOING TO DO??!!' And they would say, 'Democracy must be defended.'

The Soviets were firmly rooted in the abstract, had both their feet planted in the air. It was impossible to get them to understand that government isn't a philosophical concept, it's a utility, a service industry – a way to get roads built and have Iraqis killed. Talking politics to Soviets gave me the same dull headache that I'd had, back in college, reading *Anna Karenina*. There was Tolstoi gibbering for pages about the Russian peasant's spiritual relationship to yackitty-yackitty-yack and me going, 'Leo, why'd she fuck the guy?'

By the time I got done with the interview at the TV station, I was surrounded by two or three hundred pushing, crowding eavesdroppers. The men and boys were armed. I thought civilians didn't have guns in the Soviet Union, but I was wrong. There are liberals who have nightmares about the NRA, and those nightmares look like this crowd. Every kind of firearm imaginable was being waved around with brainless gusto. There were ancient shotguns and decrepit hunting rifles, rusty burp guns from World War II and broom-handle Mauser pistols that looked like they'd been buried in the yard since the revolution. There were scatterguns and target rifles and air pistols and hundreds of AK-47s. I saw a twelve-year-old carrying one of these. He was guarding the place where the mob had parked its cars. (Remember, this was a mob of urban elites.) I'm actually a member of the NRA and it was still a nightmare. The Second Amendment says the people have a right to 'keep and bear arms' not a right to wildly swing, waggle in your face, mispoint, stare down the barrel of and accidentally discharge the things. (Somebody did do that, fortunately into a flower bed.)

'Just what,' I said to Nina, 'is going on here? What are you people trying to accomplish? What gives?'

Nina, who was very pro-anti-Gamsakhurdia, repeated all the complaints against the man. 'But,' she said, 'in reality the problem is our president is not acting rationally. He behaves in a hysterical manner. He is crazy.'

'Crazy?' I said. 'Is that all? Nina, in the United States we elect crazy presidents all the time. You people really *don't* understand democracy, do you?'

The pro-Gamsakhurdia protesters, gathered in their own mob in front of the National Government Building, had fewer guns but seemed more dangerous – that is, more likely to beat you up instead of talk you to death.

The peasants and factory workers who supported the government were angry rather than indignant. And they'd come a long way for the purpose of being angry. On close inspection they were easy enough to distinguish from the urban elites. The pro-Gamsakhurdia protesters were older, thicker-limbed and fewer-toothed. Their clothes were the same but smellier. They were sleeping on their buses or the street and being fed free bread and pieces of dense, salty goat cheese. A movie theater had been requisitioned so they could use the rest rooms as wash stalls.

The Gamsakhurdia supporters looked satisfied enough with their accommodation. The lines for food and toilets were shorter than most lines in the Soviet Union. I watched one magnificent old man snoring on the neoclassical portico of the Government Building. He was dressed in a wrinkled suit with World War II campaign ribbons on the jacket pocket. He had shoulders as wide as a wingback chair, hands like Kool-Aid pitchers and his huge head of white hair was pillowed on a four-foot cudgel.

These were the same kind of poor, benighted slobs who supported Noriega in Panama, Pinochet in Chile, Marcos in the Philippines and Nixon during Watergate. They were mindlessly patriotic and full of ignorance and prejudices. The people at the TV station were much more like us. They really cared about human rights and social justice and even ecology, too. They were hip. They were smart. And they were wrong. The president had been duly elected. He hadn't done anything terribly unconstitutional. In fact, by the standards of the Soviet Union, he hadn't done anything worth mentioning. When, at the TV station, I'd interviewed Nodar Notadze, leader of the anti-Gamsakhurdia opposition in the Georgian Parliament, Notadze had said, 'There is no legal ground to demand his resignation. But there is moral ground.' The anti-Gamsakhurdia protesters were so smart, so hip and so much like us that you just knew, as soon as freedom and democratic government really were established in Georgia, they'd be voting for Jerry Brown.

Not that the anti-Gamsakhurdia protesters were as wimpy as Jerry Brown voters yet. Wednesday morning, 25 September, at 3 a.m. again, they tried to destroy the Tibilisi electric-power system, killing three pro-Gamsakhurdia National Guardsmen and getting two of themselves killed in the attack.

I could hear it happening – the unmistakable 'Buddha-Buddha' of AK-47 fire. I got out of bed and went rushing around the empty streets of Tibilisi looking for some sign of panic or alarm. Then I tried to call the other foreign reporters in the city, but the phone in my hotel room had a large label reading:

You are being served by Kvazy-Electronic telephone station 'KVANT'.
– Do not lift the receiver while it rings!
– Do not delay dialing!
– Do not depress the lever on the phone!

And so forth. I gave up.

It wasn't until ten in the morning that I found the site of the shooting. It was on a suburban side street, an unprepossessing structure with bullet holes and lots of shattered glass. A very rattled night manager named Jemal Bibileishvili was still behind his desk. 'I do not understand what they wanted,' he said. 'We do not control anything here.'

It turned out the anti-Gamsakhurdia protesters had attacked the office of the electric company's maintenance dispatcher. 'There is nothing here but a telephone,' said the night manager. I asked him if he could think of any possible reason for the protesters to attack this particular building. 'No,' he said, 'only, when power goes out, this is the place everyone comes to protest.'

There's a joke people tell in the Soviet Union: Mitterand, Bush and Gorbachev have a meeting with God. Mitterand says, 'My country faces many difficult problems – lagging exports, Muslim minorities, European unification. How long will it be before France's problems are solved?' God says, 'Fifteen years.' Mitterand begins to cry. 'I'm an old man,' says Mitterand. 'I'll be dead by then. I'll never see France's problems solved.' Then Bush says, 'My country faces many difficult problems – recession, crime, racial prejudice. How long will it be before America's problems are solved?' God says, 'Ten years.' Bush begins to cry. 'I'm an old man,' says Bush. 'I'll be out of office by then. I won't get any credit for solving America's problems.' Then Gorbachev says, 'My country faces many, many difficult problems. How long will it be before the Soviet Union's problems are solved?' *God begins to cry.*

IT'S THE
END OF HISTORY,
AND POLY SCI ISN'T
EXPECTED TO
RECOVER EITHER

Hearts and Minds

Shhh, they think they won the war.

The old communists who run Vietnam believe they defeated imperialism, colonialism and decadent western capitalism. So where did the little girl in Hoan Kiem park, in the middle of downtown Hanoi, get a hula hoop? Why does every house in the city have a workshop, store or tea parlor in the front room? Whence the hundreds of tiny factories? Wherefore the hawkers, barkers, jobbers and drummers shouting their wares in the street? How come foreign investors pack the haute cuisine restaurants? How come there's haute cuisine? And what is that eminently imperialist corporation, British Petroleum, doing signing a co-venture agreement with the state-owned Vietnamese oil company in the lobby of my hotel? With an open bar?

After the signing, pyrotechnics were ignited to drive away evil spirits. Twenty-foot strings of firecrackers hung from the hotel balcony. The explosions were forceful. I kept thinking about all the effort I put into dodging the draft. Now I was going to die in Vietnam anyway, twenty years late, from a stray cherry bomb.

When that famous last helicopter left the roof of the American embassy in Saigon in 1975, we were – imperially, colonially and capitalistically speaking – just going out for a beer. Now we're back. Actually *we're* not back. The United States still has some snit-induced total embargo on trade with Vietnam. But everybody else is back – French, British, Japanese, Taiwanese, Hong Kong Chinese, Mainland Chinese, overseas Vietnamese and smelly Scandinavian backpackers. Meanwhile the locals have let go of Karl Marx with both hands.

I'd come to Vietnam with photographer John Giannini who speaks Vietnamese and has been in and out of the country for most of a generation. He served two combat tours with the US Army, returned as a journalist, lived in pre-communist Saigon, got wounded during the Khmer Rouge take-over of Cambodia and – John being as persistent as Rambo sequels – came back to Vietnam again after the fall of the South. He'd been in Hanoi, last, in 1990 and warned me that, although so-called Ho Chi Minh City was coming to life, the North remained a typical People's Republic locale – short on everything except lines to stand in, dull, gray, glum, 'a big slab of drab'.

But Hanoi had definitely changed. On first impression it seemed like 1960s America – not pot, war and hirsute aggravation 60s America, but the madras-clad, record hop, beach-bunny nation of my high school days. Of course Hanoi, with its crumbling tropical seventh *arrondissement* architecture and dilapidated boulevards shaded by enormous tamarind trees, couldn't look less like midwestern suburbia. And everyone was working instead of doing the hully-gully. Nevertheless there was a doo-ron-ron in the air. Hanoi is a young city. More than half the people in Vietnam are under twenty and cheerful with the infinite possibilities of baby-boom cheer. These kids wear jeans. They wear T-shirts with catch phrases in English (sort of in English –

'Darling Pigeon/My Peacful Mind' and 'A Life's Beach'). And they ride Honda 50s just like we did. The coffee-can exhaust note, the 2-cycle gas smell, the wind-up-toy gear racket are exactly the same as they were in Ohio the summer 'Little Honda' was a top forty hit.

The streets of Hanoi are thronged with hundreds of these motor bikes and thousands of pedal-operated *cyclo* rickshaws and tens of thousands of bicycles. All are preposterously overloaded. I saw four schoolgirls on one Honda seat, a hundred cartons of something lashed to a single bicycle and ten adults and children – I counted twice – packed into and hanging off a *cyclo*.

Everyone seems to be making, selling or accomplishing something or hurrying someplace to do so. The most modest resources suffice to start a business. At every intersection old ladies hunker next to bicycle pumps, selling tire air. There aren't many black pajamas to be seen and some that I did see I suspect were Armanis. There are no long Bolshevik files of people either. The only lines I saw were lines of *cyclo* drivers waiting for fares outside restaurants and hotels. Gasoline itself is readily available – this unheard of in a Marxist country; 93 octane unleaded sells for $1.04 a gallon. It even seemed to be a buyer's market at the Ho Chi Minh Mausoleum with short, fast-moving queues to see the dead guy.

A wealth of construction is underway, mostly private houses. These are only one room wide but as much as sixty feet deep and three or four stories high. They're built of fired clay blocks or of rubble framed between poured concrete uprights. Exteriors are bright-painted stucco with mozaic decorations. Porticos, balusters, cornices and roof crestings are given shapes as fantastic and modern as the simple building materials allow. The effect is Frank Lloyd Wright in Lego blocks.

Our government translator and guide, a young foreign service officer I'll call Pham, said property is expensive in central Hanoi. Pham had no idea what the city's many 'Heroic Workers' and

'People's Victory' monuments commemorate. He had to go up and read the plaques like anyone else. But he knew to the penny – or, rather, to the karat – what real estate costs: one ounce of gold per square meter, payment in bullion only.

A government department store, the Universal State Shop, still exists, but 'steerers' hover at every counter. These are young men who tell you how you can find better, cheaper merchandise in the private shops which pay them to stand there. The steerer in the bicycle department said, quite loudly, that bikes made by the Vietnamese state monopoly cost too much, $30 to $35. He could get us a smuggled Chinese bicycle for half that price.

The private vendors in the vast, glazed-roof, trainless train-station central market have spices, vegetables, fruits, poultry and fish in profusion. I stumbled over a yard-wide wire basket filled with a python. 'God, what's that,' I said.

'Food,' said Pham.

But a large part of the Hanoi market – and of every other market in Vietnam – is given over to tools. Pipe threaders, die cutters, soldering irons, calipers and micrometers are for sale along with the usual third world hoe blades and axe heads. Plus there are all kinds of motor parts and bits of electrical and even electronic hardware. The marketplace is devoted not just to things but to things that make things. It's an industrial revolution in its nonage – like seeing young Thomas Watt stare at a boiling kettle or watching a callow Thomas Alva Edison get a shock after petting the cat.

Plenty of consumer goods are sold, too – clothes, shoes, clocks, thermos bottles, dishes, kitchen utensils – cheap but serviceable products of mainland China. Giannini said the pots and pans used to be made by hand in Hanoi. He wondered if Chinese imports had put people out of work. We drove a few blocks to Hang Thiec, 'Tin Street', but found everyone fully employed. The tinsmiths were spread out across the sidewalks and had laid sheets of corrugated metal in the road to be flattened by passing cars and trucks. Men banged on various objects with a noise like a thousand skateboarders on the roof of a quonset hut. One fellow was hammering out a medium-sized rectangular thing

63

the purpose of which escaped us. 'What's that?' asked Giannini.
'Ice cube tray!' said the artisan.

Of course the place is a dictatorship. You can do what you want, but you can't have opinions. Vietnam is still a very poor country, however. Most Vietnamese can't afford a subscription to *The New Republic* and are too busy working to watch 'Crossfire'. So there aren't that many opinions around.

It's too late for opinions anyway. The night after the British Petroleum signing, John and I were leaving our hotel when the foreign minister of China walked into the lobby. He was fresh from a first-ever meeting with his Vietnamese counterpart, and the two were giving a press conference in the banquet room. We peeked through the doorway. Everybody in there was Chinese or Vietnamese, but the press conference was being translated into English. That night, listening to the BBC World Service on shortwave, we heard Vietnam is sending food aid to the former Soviet Union. And two weeks later in Saigon – which no one pretends to call Ho Chi Minh City – I watched a young man make model airplanes out of beer cans. He folded the aluminum into carefully detailed bar room origami – C-130 transports, F-4 Phantoms, Huey and Cobra helicopters and one triangle-shaped jet with a star embossed on each wing. 'Soviet?' I said.

'No, no Soviet,' he said. But it looked like a Mig-21.

'Soviet?' I repeated.

And he pulled out a much-fingered US military plane spotter's-guide, older than he was, and pointed to a picture of this plane, a General Dynamic F-106 Delta Dagger. 'No Soviet,' he said. 'All American. Soviet no good.'

The North

A pleasant flurry of economics spreads from town all through the fields of the Hong River valley. Every garden plot is tended with the kind of care westerners wouldn't give a bonsai tree. This pays, to judge by the Hondas in the farm yards. And the same gaudy, perpendicular Hanoi houses rise from the middle of rice paddies like misplaced cubism exhibits.

We drove east to Ha Long Bay on the Tongkin Gulf. The Hong River delta has only a few bridges. The Soviets and the Chinese collaborated to build an enormous one, but they built it where there isn't any traffic. We crossed a Hong tributary, the Peaceful Time River, on a listing barge. Our car was surrounded with peasants, all of them spitting something – sugar cane pulp, sunflower seed hulls, betel nut juice – like 200 high-school juniors making their first try at dipping snuff. The barge was nudged across by a Chinese tugboat. The tug looked to have been sunk and raised several times. Running it was a position of social consequence. The captain was dressed in a three-piece suit and fedora and flew a large red flag made of painted burlap.

At Bai Chay Town on Ha Long Bay the mountains rise immediately from the riverine plain the way papier mâché tunnels used to on O-gauge train layouts. These dolomite and limestone promontories are eroded into whimsical towers, looking like the mountains on Chinese scroll paintings, as well they might since they served as models for many of those paintings.

The mountains continue directly into the sea giving Ha Long Bay some 3000 islands which are in fact the tips of mountain peaks. Waves have further eroded the limestone so that each island is wider above the high tide mark than it is at water level. Many of the islands are named after the strange resulting shapes – Teapot Island, Head Island, Turtle Island. And you can go on naming them yourself – Large Order of Fries with a Big Mac Island, Overturned Car Island, Tip of My Dick in the Bathtub Island, etc.

We hired a wooden boat, some thirty feet long and powered by a Chinese diesel engine with a single cylinder the size of a waste paper basket and r.p.m.'s so low that you could hear each stinking detonation in the combustion chamber. We motored at dog-walking speed into a flat and misty ocean. Wooden junks with their fish fin sails were becalmed in the distance, and all around us were woven basket boats or coracles hardly bigger than front hall rugs. Fishing families live in these year-round, going to bed under a roof of bowed matting and coming ashore only to sell their catch and get fresh water.

'They have lots of children,' said Pham. 'Not much else to do.' But I didn't see more than two children in any basket boat so maybe they lose a lot of children overboard, too.

The little islands, few of them more than ten acres, were covered in gnarls of vegetation. Every island seemed to have a cove and a sea arch, a little beach and a cave. One cave opened at the water line like a whale sneer, stalactite-toothed and deep enough to hide everybody in a Scout troop who wanted to sneak a smoke.

Three thousand oriental Neverlands. It was a scene of incredible beauty and hence annoyance to a journalist. Journalists aren't much good with scenic beauty. The scenic beauty story has too many unattributed sources and is short on sexual scandal. Besides, Americans have lots of questions about Vietnam and two of those questions aren't 'Is it pretty?' and 'Did you have fun?'

It is. I did. An old woman skulling a coracle came alongside and sold us ten quarts of Chinese beer. We puttered for hours, wholly content, returning to shore only in the last moments of an immense red-gold sunset so beautiful that it reduced journalists to total silence. Temporarily.

Back in Hanoi, Pham dutifully took us to Ho Chi Minh's home, a simple, open, tile-roof affair built in the Thai mountain tribesman style. It's little more than a gazebo, really, with two small rooms surrounded by a veranda upstairs and with nothing but a patio underneath. On the patio is a conference table with three telephones, and here Ho used to sit and run the whole Vietnam war. Ho Chi Minh adopted this spartan style of life in order to devote all his energy to Marxist/Leninist revolution. It makes you think better of Imelda Marcos.

Ho's house, Ho's tomb and a Ho Museum are all contained in a large park, a sort of Six Flags Over Ho with several nice ponds but no water slides into them.

The museum is supposed to be a monument to world socialism. It was designed by an unperestroikaed Czech architect working with ferroconcrete in the pre-post-modernist style – all needless parabolas, ramps to nowhere and soaring spaces that don't contain anything.

The gift shop had a display of stuffed carcasses of various animals which are nearing extinction in Vietnam. These were 'for sale to benefit endangered species'.

The exhibits were confusing. One seemed to detail the history of man from the neolithic age until the time when countries all over the world – Albania, Cuba, Laos, Mongolia, Peru and Ceylon – sent souvenir gifts to Ho Chi Minh.

The American Communist Party had sent Ho a wristwatch, a gold 'Jules Jurgensen' on a leather strap. Back in the States I asked a jeweller about this brand. He said, 'It's the kind of thing you see in a catalogue. You know – "$795 List Price. Discount Price $395. This week only, $259."'

Another exhibit contained a Coca-Cola sign, a blow-up photograph of a dead US Marine, a Marilyn Monroe poster and a plaster sculpture of an Edsel grille. This was, I think, supposed to be a mixed media presentation about the failure of bourgeois materialism, but I couldn't tell for sure because the lights and sound system were broken.

No bourgeois materialism was evident at our hotel – a government guest house, actually. The place had been built and decorated in a purely Soviet spirit. The exterior walls were made of pre-formed concrete. The interior walls were painted a Bulgarian green, and each room was lit by a single six-foot fluorescent tube so that you felt like cheap merchandise in a display case, a Jules Jergensen wristwatch perhaps. But there were non-communist touches – hot water, a new bar of soap, *two* towels. And when Giannini came down with some kind of malarial frisson the room boy gave him a massage and rubbed Tiger Balm on his eyelids.

Meals were served in traditional socialist fashion – very slowly, with the courses out of order so that the jam arrived half an hour after the toast and the coffee didn't come until you'd called for the check. However, it's hard to be angry at a place that has ice-cream, beer and cigarettes on its breakfast menu. And the cooking was good.

Everywhere else in Hanoi the cooking was even better. Also cheap. Dinner for two at the best restaurant was $6. Vietnamese food is like Chinese food prepared by a great French chef. No. That would mean frog fried rice and trying to get snails out of their shells with chopsticks. Vietnamese food is like French food with wonderful Chinese . . . That isn't it either. There's no mu shu pork in sauce *Béchamel*. Though some odd things do turn up on the bill of fare:

Vaporize Sea Fish
Volcano in Raw Mixture
Fried Beep in Minute
Fish-Sound with Chicken
Tortle in Rose Souse
Creamable Eggs
Spaghetti Soup with Chicken

The last being an accurate description of the dish. But it's delicious. It's all delicious. And every meal comes with perfectly baked baguettes, the only decent bread in Asia, and cups of *café filtre*, the only drinkable coffee east of Peshawar.

Not that Giannini and I were drinking much coffee, not with Johnny Walker Red (listed on the menu as 'Scotland Whiskey Wine') available at $17 a quart and 750 ml bottles of Stolicnaya for only $1.75. After plenty of that and some surprisingly drinkable Singapore cognac, we would be pedaled to the guest house in a pair of *cyclos*, rolling through the pitch dark but still bustling streets of Hanoi, lolling around in our chairs like participants in an Alzheimer's Olympics.

We drove out of Hanoi again, heading south on Highway 1, the old colonial road to Saigon. Every bridgehead, rail crossing and flood dyke is marked by a squat, crumbling, mold-blackened rench pillbox. In the Indo-Chinese War the French managed, y means of these pillboxes, to control all the pillboxes in the do-Chinese War. Sometimes.

In Japan people drive on the left. In China people drive on e right. In Vietnam they drive on both sides. Not that it matters nce Highway 1 is a no-lane road. Vietnam seems to have abanoned not only the idea of communism but the idea of commonveal. There is no infrastructure. There are no sewers. Electricity a sometimes thing. The tap water is an instant weight loss plan one tablespoon with every meal and eat what you want. The avement on Highway 1 is so bad that you'd make better time you drove off it and sunk to your hubs in the rice paddies. But ietnam has private property now and you can't do that.

We were traveling in an old Toyota Land Cruiser wagon with olid axles and a leaf spring front end – a vehicle designed to ispel any notion of the Japanese as automotive geniuses.

Our driver, whom I'll call Vo, had been a convoy trucker on e Ho Chi Minh Trail during the war. And we could have used ome US air strikes on Highway 1's bicycles, water buffalos, notor cycles, jeepny buses, tractors, goats, dogs, children, ox arts, flocks of ducks, private automobiles and genuine Vietna- ese pot-bellied pigs, the kind fashionable Americans have for ets and we had for dinner. Vo was good – able to drive around or over) all these at 40 m.p.h. on road surfaces barely fit for valking. But an hour out of Hanoi he suddenly pulled to the side. We have a serious problem,' he said. 'We can go no further.'

'What?' we said.

'The horn is broken.'

Vo sorted through scavenged car parts at a roadside repair hed while farmers tried to sell wives to Giannini and me. Used vives. A crowd of children collected around us.

'Lien Xo! Lien Xo!' ('Soviet'), the children said.

'Ngoni My! Ngoni My!' ('American'), said John.

The children pondered that. We looked pretty scruffy. John vas obviously wrong. 'Lien Xo! Lien Xo! Lien Xo!'

This plus a couple of Moscow businessmen wearing bowling- hirt-type sport clothes and one souvenir store at China Beach

with a faded sign in Russian were all that remained of Sovi
presence.

Vo jury-rigged something that made enough noise to get u
south. Away from Hanoi, the farms are still rich but the farme
not so much so. Houses are made of straw thatch or woven stic
or, sometimes, brick. It looks like the three little pigs are the loc
architects. Except for traffic it could be any century you lik
though here and there tall bamboo poles rise with televisio
antennas lashed to the tops.

As we neared the coast the land became hilly and dotted wi
limestone formations, chimney-like cousins of the towers in F
Long Bay. The locals are breaking these up with picks and shove
– chipping away at the sights to make gravel for roads; b
anyone who's been on the roads in Vietnam would rather hav
pavement than scenery.

The country people really do wear conical hats, called *non l*
Peering down from the highway at the open-air markets in th
villages, all you can see are hundreds of these bobbing, weavin
swaying bonnets – the dancing mushrooms from *Fantasia*. On
that thought enters your head, you can never look out the c
window in Vietnam again without hearing Tchaikovsky's *Nu
cracker Suite*.

We reached Vinh, about 170 miles from Hanoi, after ten hou
of travel. We checked into another government rest house, lil
the last one but with cockroaches the size of bronzed baby shoe
'Guests are requested to dress in a regular way in hotel restaura
and bar', read a sign in English over my bed. Vinh had been th
great staging point for the Ho Chi Minh Trail supplying th
guerrillas and NVR regulars fighting in the south. But the on
evidence of that was a weed-grown freightyard where a sing
watchman was keeping an eye on abandoned railcar unde
carriages.

Below Vinh is the neck of Vietnam where the Indochine
cordillera, the *Chaine Annamitique*, runs in close parallel to th
sea. At its narrowest point, the country is only thirty miles wid

he Ho Chi Minh trail wasn't a sneaky communist invention. It's he old trade route through Laos and Cambodia to Saigon. The North Vietnamese had to either use this or come down the middle f Highway 1 like a St Patrick's Day parade.

This has always been the poorest part of Vietnam and, as the poorest parts of so many places do, it has the best views. At one pot near the Giang River the landscape fell in multicolored bands ke a fancy after-dinner drink – a layer of sea, a layer of dunes, layer each of grass shacks and gardens, a layer of bamboo-haded road, another of rice paddies and a final layer of thick, ark mountains – a *pousse-café* of beauty.

The mountains are covered in enormous growths of tropical ardwoods. Though not for long, to judge by the number of rucks we saw carrying logs the size of trailer homes. This is all overnment timbering, done to get hard currency exports.

A high lump in the coastal plain marks the DMZ, the 'Demilit-rized Zone' that used to exist between North and South Viet-am. A cow was scratching herself against a barely legible sign ommemorating the 'Vietnamese people's victory over the Mac-Namara Line'. This, if anyone remembers, was a system of highly ophisticated electronic sensors devised by JFK's Secretary of Defense and planted in the DMZ to detect North Vietnamese nfiltration – infiltration which would have been as hard to miss s 10,000 Irishmen with bagpipes and the mayor.

The food stayed good or even got better, improving in pro-ortion to the filth of the restaurants along the road. Maybe the est meal we had in Vietnam was in a sagging, cobwebbed, hree-walled shack in Dong Hoi where rats were running along he rafters and I had to step over a pig to get to the bathroom. Not that there was anything on the other side of the pig except hole in the dirt floor.

Here they brought us *cha gio*, miniature spring rolls, chicken *ho*, the 'spaghetti soup' that was on the menu in Hanoi; another oup called *bun bo hue*, made from beef and noodles and, I think, oo chili peppers; still another soup, *chanh chua dau ca*, 'sour fish oup' (the Vietnamese will turn anything into a soup, just as the Germans will turn anything into a sausage); plus pork balls and

grilled shrimp and sticky rice and regular rice and beer and te
and mineral water, all for a buck apiece.

Food is eaten by holding a bowl under your nose and pretend
ing to use chopsticks while sucking food into your mouth wit
loud slurping noises. Holding your chopsticks too close to th
tips is considered uncouth but belching, smoking, picking th
teeth and spitting on the floor are fine. It takes a while for tab
manners to return to normal after a visit to Vietnam. As my wi
pointed out.

Most of the food is dipped in, and all of the food is flavore
with, *nuoc mam*. *Nuoc mam* is made by squeezing the juice out
fish and letting it rot in a large clay vat. The resulting liqueur
diluted with water and vinegar and set in a shallow dish on eve
table – the salt, pepper, mustard, ketchup and A-1 Sauce
Vietnam. *Nuoc mam* is an acquired taste, a taste you'd bett
acquire quickly if you don't want to do a lot of gagging.

We did not have – so far as I know – any of the other loc
delicacy which is dog. It is disturbing to western sensibilities
see a wire cage full of puppies on the way to the abattoir or,
the market, to brush against a hanging hindquarter of Rove
There is that little tail which did so lately wag at master. 'Si
'Fetch!' 'Shake hands!' 'Now jump in the frying pan!' 'Good dog

We arrived in Hue, on the Perfume River, at sunset. Hue wa
the imperial capital of Vietnam, famous for its two-square-mi
fortress, the Citadel. This was built by the Emperor Gai Long
1804 but never saw any actual fortress use until the 1968 T
offensive and then the Viet Cong attackers got on the wrong sid
of the walls and held out in there for twenty-four days.

Inside the Citadel is the impressive Palace of Supreme Ha
mony. Though what impresses you, really, is the unfamiliari
of the decorations – the dragon tangles carved into the woo
work, ,the Parcheesi board patterns in the screens and railin
and the old-shoe-in-the-closet turned-up tips of the roof corner
Once you've looked at it awhile you realize that the Palace
Supreme Harmony is squatty and dank and not a patch on th
average Grand Hyatt.

Hue is also famous for beautiful women though all of Vietnam has them and not just singular enchantresses but huge aggregate percentages of sirens and belles. Any random group of thirty Vietnamese women will contain a dozen who make Cindy Crawford look like Ross Perot. In the early evening in Hue the girls from the secondary schools come home from classes, fleets of them bicycling through the streets, all dressed in white *oa dais*, trim shirt dresses worn over loose-fitting trousers. Not for nothing do the remaining Catholic churches ring the *angelus* this time of day. I wonder if it changes the nature of a society for beauty to be so common. Maybe in Vietnam 'she has a wonderful personality' really means something. But I couldn't figure out a polite way to ask.

We left for Da Nang at dawn. Driving in the dark is impossible in Vietnam, so we had reverted to the visceral body clock of the medieval serf – passed out in the vermin by nine and up before five. Thirty-five miles south of Hue we drove up an astounding set of switchbacks, un-guard-railed and rapidly coming unpaved, our precarious roadbed crossing and recrossing the equally precarious roadbed of Vietnam's single railway line.

Then Vo wheeled us down at a startling angle onto a coast of little shining harbors and cheddar-colored beaches arrayed in quarter moons and trefoils between rocky headlands. Thatch villages sat in palm groves between the ocean and the road, emerald gardens opened out to the west. Either Eden looked like this or Eve was right to back the snake.

Now I understand how we got involved in Vietnam. We fell in love. Maybe the grunts didn't. They had to look at too much incoming and too many other grunts. But the big shots we sent there – the suits, the brass hats, the striped pants cookie pushers, the CIA white shoe boys and the special envoy face cards – they swooned for the place. Everybody, from the first advisers Ike sent in 1955 to Henry Kissinger at the Paris Peace talks, had a mad crush on Vietnam. It broke their hearts. They kept calling and sending flowers. They just couldn't believe this was goodbye.

Qua Roi

It's been nineteen years now US newspapers, magazines and television programs weren't, in 1964, filled with agonizing reappraisals of World War II. I'd like to be the first American to write something about Vietnam without having kittens. I wasn't in the war. I didn't lose my youth and innocence here. (I lost them the regular way, with a calendar.) don't feel guilty about dodging the draft. Well, maybe a little but I'm forty-four years old and, by now, I've done a lot of things to feel guilty about. Ducking conscription into a dubious military venture is way down the list. Yes, I had friends who died here But I had friends who died from cocaine and I don't get all weird every time I see a glass-topped coffee table.

'*Qua roi*', 'past enough', is what the Vietnamese say when you ask them about the war. Our battles in Vietnam are as remote in time for the majority of Vietnamese as our battles in Korea are for me (if Korea had taken place on my block, of course). To look at Vietnam, you'd never know there'd been a war. Giannini said the farmers used to use bomb craters to raise catfish. But since price controls on rice were lifted, the craters have been filled and smoothed into the surrounding paddies. I heard that damage from the defoliant Agent Orange lingers in some places, though how you'd tell it from government lumbering I don't know. U airbases stand fenced-off and unused in Da Nang and Tuy Hoa the rocket-proof hangars looking like upside-down poker chip trays. The great strategic jackpot of southeast Asia, Cam Ranh Bay, contained exactly one freighter, rusting and locally regis tered. On a scrap heap south of Hue I saw two empty napalm pods stenciled 'U.S.A.F'. I saw a Mig fighter plane kiddie carrou sel in Vinh. In Hai Phong a ruined street has been preserved to commemorate the 1972 'Christmas Bombing' which President Nixon launched to remind the North Vietnamese to pay attention at the negotiating table. But when Pham and Vo asked around in Hai Phong, nobody could recall where the street was.

John and I had gone to the War Museum in Hanoi. Its main

courtyard is filled by a ziggurat of American plane wreckage – a Hellcat supplied to the French in the 50s, some kind of pilotless drone from 1965, an F-111 shot down in 1972 and large sections of a B-52 intercepted that same year. Perched on top, all in one piece, is a North Vietnamese Mig-21. This is supposed to be a triumphal display, but it only succeeds in looking like the pile of waste that it is.

Inside the museum just a few of the galleries are dedicated to what we think of as the War in Vietnam. Displays are arranged chronologically. The first exhibit concerns Trung Trac and Trung Nhi, sisters who led a rebellion against Chinese colonists in 40 AD. Thus the Vietnamese had 1,923 more years of experience in guerrilla warfare than the US Army did. The largest exhibit is a scale model of the valley at Dien Bien Phu, a miniature landscape as big as a tennis court showing, in precise detail, just how dumb were the French.

In the room devoted to the American era there are huge photos of US college students protesting the war policies of President 'Gion Xon'. I couldn't actually find my own face in any of the pictures, but close enough. A little embarrassing – it's one thing for me to be nostalgic about hippie days and something else for commie dictators to celebrate my past.

And then the museum just keeps going – fall of the South Vietnamese government in 1975, expulsion of Pol Pot from Phnom Penh in 1978, border clashes with the Chinese in 1979. When,' I asked Pham, 'was the last period of sustained peace in Vietnam?'

'Oh, seventeenth, eighteenth century,' he said.

The only thing the Vietnamese seem to have against America now is that we won't do business with them, won't open our markets, won't let them make money off us the way everybody else in Asia does. (Won't, that is, not counting the thousands I was paying the Vietnamese government for this grand tour.)

The problem is, of course, POWs and MIAs. As of 1 July 1991, 2,266 Americans are unaccounted for in Southeast Asia. Of

these 650 are believed to have been captured alive. John and
had dinner with one of the people from the US government'
Office for POW/MIA Affairs in Hanoi. He believes it's possibl
that American POWs are still alive in Vietnam. He doesn't thin
it's likely, but the Vietnamese government is morally capable o
a thing like that. 'Live Americans are political chips,' he said
'Dead Americans are economic chips.'

The sad thing is that political chips aren't worth much no
the cold war is gone. It would be embarrassing for a live America
to show up in Vietnamese custody at this late date. I personall
have a bad feeling that, if any American POWs were alive, th
Vietnamese government killed them. We're not dealing wit
Vaclev Havel here.

The dead bodies of Americans, however, are definitely bein
held in Vietnam. The Vietnamese government may be warehous
ing remains as some kind of bargaining ploy – nobody knows
But we do know that the peasants and mountain tribesmen i
remote parts of Vietnam have some bones and dog-tags. Amer
can pilots wore, sewn into their flight suits, something know
as a 'blood chit'. It said – in Vietnamese, French, English, Laotiar
Kamchukian and other languages – that the US governme
would reward anyone who returned that pilot. People in rura
Vietnam are caught between greed and fear. They believe the
will be given money and help in emigrating if they return Amer
can remains to Americans (which isn't true). And they belie
they will be in trouble if their government catches them tryin
this (which is true). So the farmers and hill folks hoard these sa
and grisly artifacts. And the men from the US Office of POW
MIA Affairs travel all over Vietnam tracking down rumors an
leads.

One night at dinner Vo and Giannini discovered they'd been o
opposite sides of the same series of battles along the Cambodia
border in the early 70s – something they both seemed to thin
was very amusing. A large number of toasts were drunk. Phan
who was too young to fight Americans, and I, who was a long

aired peace creep, were left out. John and Vo filled their glasses
rst with beer, then with Scotch, then with a terrifying rice
hiskey called *ba xi de*. 'One hundred per cent!' Vo would shout,
e Vietnamese call for a chug-a-lug. '*Di di mau!*' John would
out, which means 'get the hell out of here'. And they'd drain
eir drinks in a gulp. They got quite merry. And so did the
staurant owners, happily totaling the check.

The South

It was the first full moon of the
nar new year, an auspicious day. New fishing boats were being
unched into the harbor at Da Nang with so many good luck
reworks that these boats would never sink, they'd blow up. We
ent down the coast a few miles to the old port town of Hoi An,
center of Vietnam's ethnic Chinese, or Hoa. They number 1.3
illion, or did before 1975 when many became 'boat people'.
he Hoa were merchants and manufacturers. They were very
ccessful and thus, according to the logic of Marxism, respon-
ble for society's failures. The Hoa suffered the same fate as the
zza parlor owner in Spike Lee's *Do the Right Thing* except at the
ands of the world's fourth largest army instead of a small,
etulant movie director.

But most Hoa stuck it out. On this day they'd come to Hoi
n's pagodas to pay respects to their ancestors. We saw our first
vilian Mercedes-Benz here and several Honda Accords. New
othes and big jewelry abounded. We visited a house on the
uay along the Thu Bon River, built in the eighteenth century
nd occupied by the same family of Hoa merchants for seven
enerations. These tradesmen had survived the radical leveling
f the 1771 Tay Son Rebellion (slogan: 'Seize the property of the
ch and distribute it to the poor'), the ridiculous taxes of the
bsequent Nguyen Dynasty, the thefts and depredations of
rench colonialism, the worse thefts and greater depredations of
panese occupation, the amazing corruption of the Ngo Dinh

Diem regime, the drunks and diddlings of American soldiers an
the all-of-the-aboves of communism.

The long, dark interior of the house was dense with orn
ment, its walls carved and lacquered like an inside-out reliquar
The exterior looked – wisely enough – like nothing much.

Vo had to go back to Hanoi. We got a second, and very ba
driver to take us on to Saigon. We went along the coast, pa
the fabulous expanse of China Beach where there's no trace
Americans, not even actress litter such as wadded-up divor
rulings or left-over nose jobs. A quack doctor was giving a sho
by the roadside. He held forth with the wide gestures and spee
cadences universal to his type. But humbug is improved by ign
ance of the language. ' . . . relieves Marxist/Leninism!' perha
the quack was saying. 'Purges collectivist thinking! Relieves ce
tral planning! An unfailing antidote and panacea – it will ev
cure socialized medicine!'

South of Da Nang the villages were small – grass shacks
the beaches with terraced fields cut out of the hills on the oth
side of the highway. Despite the heavy traffic the farmers lea
sliced sweet potatoes on the road to dry in the sun – swe
potatoes in a light asphalt sauce finished with truck tire. There
no other place to put the crop. Only 20 per cent of Vietnam
land is flat enough to farm. And that 20 per cent is some of t
most densely populated acreage in the world. You're never o
of sight of people. And this is a problem if you want privacy f
certain body functions.

Traveling in the third world entails an extraordinary amou
of having to go to the bathroom. And right now. I've read a l
of travel writing and never seen this mentioned. T.E. Lawren
does touch on bowel movements in *Seven Pillars of Wisdom*, b
that's war reporting and, anyway, he was constipated whi
hardly counts. The irresistible food and unmentionable hygie
of Vietnam make a particularly bad combination. And no amou
of Lomotil, Pepto Bismol or quick trips over the top of restaura
pigs seemed to do any good. Between Da Nang and Na Tran;
actually found a gas station with a decent john. It was a Turkis

squatter-style toilet in a dark, damp room. But it didn't smell and it had toilet paper instead of the usual small jug of water. I got my jeans around my ankles and was just hunkering down when I spied movement. I stood up and lit a match. The toilet was full to the brim with crawling insects, uncountable numbers of them, each as big as a Bic lighter.

Even when I didn't have to go to the bathroom I felt like I did. My kidneys were swinging around like twin tether balls during the fourteen hours a day of jolting in the Land Cruiser, and my prostate was swollen to the size of a paperback book. Actually this was a welcome distraction from back pain. My spine felt like a stack of broken china. But, since we were getting up at five, no discomfort was too severe to keep me from dozing off. Then the car would drop into an abysmal pot hole and my sleeping face would be sent on a long arc into the dashboard.

Fortunately Giannini and I were adhering to the two key rules of third world travel:

1. Never run out of whiskey.
2. Never run out of whiskey.

We were also calling frequent halts so we could make notes or take pictures. We were willing to do anything, even our jobs, to get out of the car.

We stopped in a village called Xuan Tho where the men were all building a wooden boat like the one we'd used in Ha Long Bay. The timber had been cut locally. The keel, transom, gunwales and other specially named pieces of boat wood were being shaped by hand. One man squatted by a whetstone doing nothing all day but sharpening adzes and chisels. There was one power tool, an electric drill hooked up to the village's small generator. Bolts, washers and nuts were the only machine-made parts in the hull, and there were only a few of these. The rest of the boat was being put together with wedges and pegs. The whole, including cabin and fittings, would cost about $2000, but then they'd have to pay $3500 for a Chinese diesel. It won't be long before they hear about outboards. By the time I get back to Vietnam they'll be skiing behind this boat.

We stopped at another village to watch a fight. The long wooden yokes used to carry coolie baskets turn out to double as quarter staffs – in case anyone wants to do multicultural casting of Little John in the next Robin Hood remake.

And we stopped in yet another village to look at circus posters. Most of the acts seemed to involve severed heads or girls in tight clothing being pierced by knives, plus some levitation and swallowing of razor blades. The circus posters were propped against a wall, obscuring a communist propaganda mural. The figures in the mural – a worker, a peasant, a soldier and so forth – were staring off into the distance. People in communist propaganda art are always staring off into the distance. Did they just cut one?

Giannini tried to talk to everybody we met – so we wouldn't have to get back in the Land Cruiser. But he didn't have much success. John speaks with a Saigon accent and Vietnamese regional pronunciation varies greatly. I had a little book called, tellingly, *Vietnamese So Easy!* I didn't even try. Vietnamese is tonal so that meaning varies not only according to the sound you make but according to whether you make that sound as a tenor or a baritone. *Cho*, *cho* and *cho* mean, with tonal variations of the vowel, 'market', 'dog' and 'to give'. The rest of the language is just as phonetically subtle. *Com* (cooked rice), *khong* (no), *cam* (orange), *ca'm* (not allowed) and *kem* (ice-cream) are all pronounced, to the American ear, 'kum'. Thus you can ask somebody to give you ice-cream and wind up in the market with a forbidden orange dog.

We stayed the night in Na Trang, another of Vietnam's exasperating number of beauty spots. The little harbor here is tucked between mountains. Bright blue fishing boats ride at anchor, gimlet eyes painted on their bows. A miniature shrine to the sea gods sits on the harbor rock. And a seventh-century Cham tower commands the scene, the Cham being an indigenous people of Hindu beliefs who built sandstone monuments in chocolate-dipped Dairy Queen shapes.

It is a photograph damned to endless appearance in tourist brochures. And, indeed, the French are planning a Club Med in Na Trang. The French will then accomplish, with sexually transmitted diseases, what they failed to do with soldiers and rubber plantations.

Rubber plantations were what made the French so intent on keeping Indochina – lest the Michelin Man have to go around in a barrel. Rubber plantations seem like an odd idea. It's hard not to imagine the woods full of tire swings, or worse. In fact they look like any forest except the trees are in perfect rows – as if God had, for one moment during creation, been spelled by a certified public accountant.

In between the rubber plantations were hop yards for Vietnam's excellent beer and vineyards for Vietnam's execrable wine and mango trees smelling like perfume on your high-school girlfriend.

We turned inland at Phan Thiet. The hills here, at the end of the dry season, are sere and almost Mexican looking. Old American and European cars began to appear on the road. The mile markers all read 'Saigon' now instead of being painted over with the abbreviation for Ho Chi Minh City. Buddhist monks wandered around with their begging bowls – almost as many as in Boulder, Colorado. Churches were open and I saw a new Catholic church being built.

Saigon doesn't begin at any particular place. It just oozes out of the surrounding country until you realize the farms are gone and you're circled by industrial litter. Billboards advertise Taiwanese electronics and Japanese cameras. And traffic is heavy enough to bring itself to a halt, something that doesn't happen anywhere else in Vietnam. There are four stoplights in the 1,050 miles between Hanoi and Saigon, and only the one in Saigon is being obeyed and that only because the intersection is blocked. Here, finally, is something other than a beauty spot. Saigon has none of rural poverty's loveliness, none of manual labor's charm. Saigon is like all the other great modern cities of the world. It's the mess left from people getting rich.

Hearts and Minds and Wallets

Never has there been such pure, unconcealed all-hogs-to-the-trough capitalism among the citizens of a supposedly collectivist milieu. (Never, that is, if you don't count the drug and tie-dye bazaars in the parking lots outside Greatful Dead concerts.) The Vietnamese government had been edging towards economic reform since the late 70s. But nothing seemed to work. Whatever the government tried, the country remained a socialist butthole. Then, about a year and a half ago, the commies just gave up. They took the price controls off everything, put privacy back into private property and told everybody to go make a living. Faced with a choice between leading and following, the Vietnamese government got out of the way. And the Vietnamese people aren't Russians. They didn't just stand there with their dong in their hands. (Dong is, no joke, what the money's called. $1 US = 11,500 dong. As Claudia Rosset, editorial page editor of the *Asia Wall Street Journal*, has pointed out, the first thing the Vietnamese have to do, if they're serious about being a credible part of the world economy, is change the name of their currency.)

The economic situation in Vietnam is so interesting that I was almost interested in talking to economists. I interviewed Do Duc Dinh whose business card read, 'Head of Developing Countries Economic Study Department, Institute of World Economy, National Center for Social Sciences of Viet Nam' – a title almost as long as one of those articles in the *New York Review of Books* excusing the failure of Marxism. Speaking of which, Mr Do is firmly against central planning. The people who generate central planning's abstract theories are no longer important, he said. 'You may think of sky,' said Mr Do, 'and not know sky. You may think earth looks like sky.'

Where this left the Institute of World Economy and its Developing Countries Economic Study Department, I didn't ask. But wasn't Mr Do – as a nominal marxist, or employee of nominal marxists, or, anyway, public official in a country with a famous dead marxist stuffed and exhibited for veneration – worried about capitalist exploitation of the masses? 'People were afraid if the window was opened flies and mosquitoes would come in,' said Mr Do. 'But with money we can buy mosquito repellant or screens.'

Le Dang Doanh, Deputy Director of the Central Institute for Economic Management, was even more emphatically against economic management being centralized in things like institutes. He told a story about a fisherman who was a Communist Party member and the head of a local fishing co-operative. The government-set price for fish was less than the cost of catching them. The other fishermen sold their fish on the black market and made a living. But the party member felt the dignity of his office and couldn't bring himself to break the law. He lost money every time he went to sea. Finally he cut off his thumb so he'd never have to fish again.

Mr Le said that in 1989 state-controlled markets were selling rice for 50 dong a kilo. When price restrictions were lifted the price increased by more than 1200 per cent. For a moment I thought Mr Le was describing the other side of the coin, that I was going to hear another story, this time about someone who cut off his thumb for food. But no. 'In one year rice production increased by one million metric tons,' said Mr Le. Vietnam, which had formerly needed to import 500,000 metric tons of rice a year, now exports 1.4 million. 'Production increased and consumption fell,' said Mr Le. But, I asked, does that mean people are going hungry? 'Ha!' said Mr Le. 'They used to stand in line to buy rice for pigs. It was cheaper than pig food.'

Mr Le – who is sometimes called, for his rhetorical style, 'Mr I-would-like-to-say' – then lectured me on the benefits of the free market. Lectured *me* – a New Hampshire tax refugee and unreconstructed country club Republican who twice voted for Ronald Reagan and will vote for him a third time this fall. Le Dang Doanh was educated in East Germany. Le Dang Doanh was an economic adviser to Truong Chinh, the hard-line former Secretary General of the Vietnamese Communist Party. And Le Dang Doanh wanted to make sure I understood economic liberty.

Next some liberal Democrat American presidential candidate will come out for a 15 per cent flat rate income tax.

American presidential candidates – that's about what Le Dang Doanh and Do Duc Dinh are. Their free market gab is all mixed – like Bill Clinton's – with calls for government programs. In fact, they and Bill are calling for government programs from the same government – ours. Le and Do want US aid in the form of IMF and World Bank loans to the Vietnamese state.

Le and Do saw nothing contradictory about pursuing free enterprise while increasing totalitarian wherewithal. Nor did a third economist, Dr Nguyen Xuan Oanh. Dr Nguyen went to Harvard and was once an official in the South Vietnamese government. He was sent to a re-education camp after the fall of Saigon but is now rehabilitated and a member of the People's Assembly. Imagine the coals-to-Newcastle problem of turning a Harvard grad into a socialist. Not that Dr Nguyen is a socialist anymore. 'If you keep on being socialist, the only way you go is down,' he said. None the less he was full of ideas for social engineering. He proposed mandating 'weaker beer' to alleviate the social chaos that might result from capitalism. Isn't it dangerous, I asked, to mix the unlimited economic power of an unregulated market with the infinite political power of an undemocratic state? Isn't this a recipe for corruption on a truly US Congressional scale? Dr Nguyen disagreed. 'I don't think it would cost much to corrupt *our* politicians – they wouldn't know what to do with large amounts of money.'

Le Dang Doanh told me that in Vietnam 'the taxation system is quite weak'. He seemed to think this was a problem. 'The state is poor but people are rich,' he said. Consider the glorious prospect of President Bush living in his car. Imagine Senators forced to panhandle for legislation. 'Spare fifty billion for a five-year omnibus farm bill?' Picture the US Attorney General driving a cab at night and the Secretary of Housing and Urban Development living in the projects. Think about the Drug Czar on drugs and Ted Kennedy trying to cash food stamps at a liquor store. Envision, if you will, 435 congressmen on street corners with hand-lettered cardboard signs: 'Will Work for Votes'.

The Light at the End of the Tunnel Is Neon

Saigon looks like it's governed by bums already. People are sleeping in doorways. Laundry hangs in the guard towers of the former US Embassy. The old architecture has long gone to seed and wasn't much to begin with, a product of 50s aesthetics and 60s communal violence – bunker modern.

Gnat packs of little kids follow you down the sidewalks shouting, 'Where you from ! Hello! You give me money!' The pedlars and shopkeepers shout at you, too, 'You buy here! Where you from! Where you from!' You wave them all away trying to say 'No! No! No!' in Vietnamese and probably saying 'Ice-cream! Cooked rice! Orange!'

Saigon is still a predominantly two-wheeled city, but motorized and not just with little Honda engines. Young idiots hardball down the avenues on 500cc café racers. Even bicycles are ridden with attitude. Traffic is like a bad dog. It isn't important to look both ways when crossing the street. It's important to not show fear.

There are many more cars here than in Hanoi. Some are new and Japanese, but there are also Citroëns and Peugeots from the 50s, Mustangs and Mercedes from the 60s and giant Chevrolets from the early 70s. The older cars are well-preserved. In 1975 the citizens of Saigon drove their automobiles through the french doors into the front parlors of their homes, turned the locks, pulled the blinds and waited until Vietnam got over communism.

John and I visited a little garage the size of the basement at your house and not much better equipped. The mechanics had one drill press, one lathe, a paint sprayer and an acetylene torch. With these, a dozen cars from Saigon's unintentional time capsule were being restored – a 1971 Peugeot 404 convertible, a little A-2 US Army jeep, a 1972 Toyota 800 sports car and so on. They're collectors items now and will all be re-exported to foreign buyers. An exquisite 1958 Citroën Traction – the getaway car of choice in twenty years of French bankrobber movies – had just been sold to someone in Italy for US $6000.

This was one of thousands of plans and schemes, projects and plots. In the rest of Vietnam people are trying to make money. In Saigon they're succeeding. Restaurants are opening by the score, none as good as the Dong Hoi roadside shack with the pig in the toilet but all with concessions to international taste such as forks, hamburgers, sit-down commodes and huge prices. It's like being in the Vietnam Pavilion at Epcot Center. There's even a bar called Apocalypse Now, decorated with war memorabilia. And plenty of American Vietnam vets are back on vacation, reeling around in shock at discovering their girlfriends have turned forty. An international Marathon had just been run in Saigon, although the Vietnamese are inexperienced in these matters and didn't think to block traffic. And the locals were so intrigued by people running without being chased that they swarmed onto the course, asking, 'Where you from!'

The apartment where the narrator in Graham Greene's *The Quiet American* smoked his opium has been torn down to make way for a 600-room hotel financed by Taiwanese. A floating hotel – which had gone into Chapter 11 on the Great Barrier Reef because Aussies prefer a drink in the room to a room in the drink – has been towed up the Saigon River. I was schmoozed by a woman in the bar there. I assumed she was a prostitute. Worse than that, she sold real estate.

'Joint venture!' is, after 'Where you from!', the most heard phrase in Saigon. Government and private citizens alike are trying to get in on them, though the government is doing so with typical communist confusion. I visited the gigantic state textile company, Legamex, which wants to turn itself into a publicly held corporation. 'The problem now,' an executive told me, 'is how to evaluate our fixed assets.' A value of what people would pay apparently not having occurred to him.

The government has also reopened Ehu Tho racetrack. The grandstands haven't been painted, or swept, since Saigon fell, and the groundskeepers seem to belong to some littering advocacy group, but Ehu Tho is filled with punters. God knows what their handicap method is. The horses are ponies, the jockeys are children and neither seem to be trained for anything particular. Just getting the kids mounted is no sure bet. They are supposed to be sixteen years old but I doubt most are twelve and some looked as young as eight. I watched one trainer hold a tyke in racing silks aloft with both hands and chase a rearing horse around the paddock, trying to slam-dunk his jockey into the saddle. In the first race only one kid had his feet placed properly in the stirrups and he ran second to last.

When the starting gate opens the horses run down the track any old way, like mice let out of a paper sack. Jockeys are launched in every direction. A riderless horse is placed third in one race. The moment the jockeys cross the finish line – or come to in the infield – they have to run back to the tack room and strip. Somebody else needs the jersey for the next race.

Di choi, 'go for fun', the atmosphere in Saigon is called. Gianinni and I tried to have some at the Super Star Disco. Unfortunately, Asia is the continent rhythm forgot. At best Asian music is off-brand American pop, like hiring your cousin's band to play the prom. At worst Asian music sounds as if a truck full of wind chimes collided with a stack of empty oil drums during a bird call contest. The locals boogied away regardless, dancing in the style of parents at a Bar Mitzvah.

Out on the streets the whores were cruising, whores on motor scooters who wear tight jeans, a pound of makeup and elbow-length blue gloves; whores being pedaled around in *cyclos* by their combination pimp/rickshaw driver boyfriends, and whores who stand outside hotel lobbies. 'Where you from! Where you from! Where you from!' There are junkies, too. They can't get needles so they slash their legs with razor blades and rub heroin into the wounds. You see them bandaged and hobbling on crutches like victims of pathetic accidents except for the slow and dreamy way they hobble.

'How is this different from Saigon before it fell?' I asked Gianinni.

'It isn't,' he said.

Hard to believe that the thrilling ideal of human liberty always ends up with people acting so . . . human. Like Americans or something. Reading *The Rights of Man*, the *Declaration of Independence*, the preamble to the *Constitution*, it's something of a disappointment to know that the fruit borne by our founding fathers' noble struggles and hard sacrifices is, um, me. Me and the Vietnamese. Ho Chi Minh, after all, called himself 'the George Washington of Vietnam'.

In the Saigon shops there are thousands of Zippo lighters left behind by US soldiers. Each lighter is engraved with a byword or motto, most often:

> OURS IS NOT TO DO OR DIE
> OURS IS TO SMOKE AND STAY HIGH

SECOND
THOUGHTS

A

SERIOUS

PROBLEM

'Is it serious?' we ask the doctor. 'I'm not kidding,' we tell the child. 'What's so funny?' says the voice of authority from classroom to army camp to editorial page of the *New York Times*. The threat of solemnity haunts our lives. Little profit and less pleasure accrue from most somber occasions. The smiles of people emerging from courtrooms, church services and even wedding ceremonies are usually smiles of relief. Life is weighty, important, grave, critical, momentous, etc. Not for nothing does *Roget's Thesaurus* say '*Antonyms* – See DRUNKENNESS, FRIVOLITY, PLAYFULNESS, UNIMPORTANCE.' Yes, indeed, let's see them right away.

But though wise men spend their days trying to stay out of serious trouble, there are other people who frankly wallow in sobriety. They look serious, think about serious things, pick serious topics and speak about them seriously. These are the dinner partners who discuss famine over oysters, the house guests who lecture infirm great-aunts on the importance of aerobic exercise, the journalists who author articles titled 'Whither Gambia' (a kind of writing known in the trade as MEGO: 'My Eyes Glaze Over'). Why do they do it?

My guess is self-loathing. Self-loathing is one of those odd, illogical leaps of human intuition that is almost always correct.

'Serious' people are dense and know it. But, they think, if they can be grave enough about Yugoslavia their gravity will make up for the fact that – like most people – they don't know what's going on there, and – like all people – they don't know what to do about it. Seriousness is stupidity sent to college.

Serious topics also make unimportant people feel as important as what they're discussing. Of course, it's necessary to make sure everyone understands how important the topic is. Hemingway was just a tourist watching Spaniards tease farm animals. But if he could make cattle-pestering a grand and tragic thing in the eyes of the public, he'd become grand and tragic too, because he'd been there while somebody did it.

Truly serious topics give this kind of bore a rare conversational advantage. There isn't any decent way to shut him up. Nobody wants to be caught saying, 'Who cares if seventy thousand people drowned in Bangladesh?'

Seriousness is also the great excuse for sin. These days anything can be forgiven if the person was sincere about his actions. 'I did what I thought was best at the time' is the modern equivalent of a perfect act of contrition. Personally, I'd be more inclined to absolve George Bush if he'd let Saddam Hussein live from pure good nature. But 'I was acting in what I felt to be the best interests of the nation' seems to be more what the public wants to hear.

Seriousness lends force to bad arguments. If a person is earnest enough about what he says, he must have *some* point. There's a movement in some of our school systems to give creationists equal time in science class. Man was plopped down on earth the week before last, is one rib short on the left, and because silly people are serious about this so are we.

Seriousness is also the only practical tone to take when lying. The phrase 'to lie with a straight face' is prolix. All lies are told with a straight face. It's truth that's said with a dismissive giggle.

Real seriousness is involuntary. If you're held at gunpoint or run over by a bus, you'll be serious about it. If you're a decent person, you'll also have some serious feelings when you see someone else threatened or squashed. In fact, if you're a decent person faced with the world's catastrophes, horrors and pleas for help, you'll do the right thing whether you're serious or not.

Sir Thomas More jested with his head on the block. 'My neck is very short,' he warned the executioner. 'Take heed, therefore, thou strike not awry, for saving of thine honesty.' The Persian king Xerxes was astonished when his scouts told him the Spartans holding the pass at Thermopylae were combing their hair and changing into clean clothes for the battle. Gallantry is the proper tone for those who are worth being taken seriously. With one exception – serious looks and serious voice are absolutely necessary when calling the dog.

SECOND THOUGHTS ABOUT THE 1960s

What I believed in the sixties

Everything. You name it and I believed it. I believed love was all you need. I believed you should be here now. I believed drugs could make everyone a better person. I believed I could hitchhike to California with thirty-five cents and people would be glad to feed me. I believed Mao was cute. I believed private property was wrong. I believed my girlfriend was a witch. I believed my parents were Nazi space monsters. I believed the university was putting saltpeter in the cafeteria food. I believed stones had souls. I believed the NLF were the good guys in Vietnam. I believed Lyndon Johnson was plotting to murder all the Negroes. I believed Yoko Ono was an artist. I believed Bob Dylan was a musician. I believed I would live forever or until twenty-one, whichever came first. I believed the world was about to end. I believed the Age of Aquarius was about to happen. I believed the *I Ching* said to cut classes and take over the dean's office. I believed wearing my hair long would end poverty and injustice. I believed there was a great throbbing web of psychic mucus and we were all part of it somehow. I managed to believe Gandhi and H. Rap Brown at the same time. With the exception of anything my mom and dad said, I believed everything.

What Caused Me to Have Second Thoughts

One distinct incident sent me scuttling back to Brooks Brothers. From 1969 to 1971 I was a member of a 'collective' running an 'underground' newspaper in Baltimore. The newspaper was called, of all things, *Harry*. When *Harry* was founded, nobody could think what to name the thing so some girl's two-year-old son was asked. His grandfather was Harry and he was calling everything Harry just then so he said, 'Harry', and *Harry* was what the paper was called. It was the spirit of the age.

Harry was filled with the usual hippie blather, yea drugs and revolution, boo war and corporate profits. But it was an easy-going publication and not without a sense of humor. The want-ads section was headlined 'Free Harry Classifieds Help Hep Cats and Kittens Fight Dippy Capitalist Exploitation'. And once when the office was raided by the cops (they were looking for mari-juana, I might add, not sedition), *Harry* published a page-one photo of the mess left by the police search. The caption read, 'Harry office after bust by pigs.' Next to it was an identical photo captioned, 'Harry office before bust by pigs.'

Our 'collective' was more interested in listening to Captain Beefheart records and testing that new invention, the water bed, than in overthrowing the state. And some of the more radical types in Baltimore regarded us as lightweights or worse. Thus, one night in the summer of 1970, the *Harry* collective was invaded by some twenty-five blithering Maoists armed with large sticks. They called themselves, and I'm not making this up, the 'Balto Cong'. They claimed they were liberating the paper in the name of 'the people'. In vain we tried to tell them that the only thing the people were going to get by liberating *Harry* was ten thousand dollars in debts and a mouse-infested row house with overdue rent.

There were about eight *Harry* staffers in the office that evening. The Balto Cong held us prisoner all night and subjected each of us to individual 'consciousness-raising' sessions. You'd be hauled off to another room where ten or a dozen of these nutcakes would sit in a circle and scream that you were a revisionist running dog imperialist paper tiger watchama-thing. I don't know about the rest of the staff, but I conceded as quick as I could to every word they said.

Finally, about 6:00 a.m., we mollified the Balto Cong by agreeing to set up a 'people's committee' to run the paper. It would be made up of their group and our staff. We would all meet that night on neutral turf at the Free Clinic. The Balto Cong left in triumph. My airhead girlfriend had been converted to Maoism during her consciousness-raising session. And she left with them.

While the Balto Cong went home to take throat pastilles and make new sticks or whatever, we rolled into action. There were, in those days, about a hundred burned-out 'street people' who depended on peddling *Harry* for their livelihood. We rallied all of these, including several members of a friendly motorcycle gang, and explained to them how little sales appeal *Harry* would have if it were filled with quotations from Ho Chi Minh instead of free-love personals. They saw our point. Then we phoned the Balto Cong crash pad and told them we were ready for the meeting. 'But,' we said, 'is the Free Clinic large enough to hold us all?' 'What do you mean?' they said. 'Well,' we said, 'we're bringing about a hundred of our staff members and there's, what, twenty-five of you, so . . . ' They said, um, they'd get back to us.

We were by no means sure the Balto Cong threat had abated. Therefore the staff photographer, whom I'll call Bob, and I were set to guard the *Harry* household. Bob and I were the only two people on the staff who owned guns. Bob was an ex-Marine and something of a flop as a hippie. He could never get the hair and the clothes right and preferred beer to pot. But he was very enthusiastic about hippie girls. Bob still had his service automatic.

I had a little .22-caliber pistol that I'd bought in a fit of wild self-dramatization during the '68 riots. 'You never know when the heavy shit is going to come down,' I had been fond of saying. Although I'd pictured it 'coming down' more from the Richard Nixon than the Balto Cong direction. Anyway, Bob and I stood guard. We stood anxious guard every night for two weeks, which seemed an immense length of time back in 1970. Of course we began to get slack, not to say stoned, and forgot things like locking the front door. And through that front door, at the end of two weeks, came a half dozen hulking Balto Cong. Bob and I were at the back of the first-floor office. Bob had his pistol in the waistband of his ill-fitting bell-bottoms. He went to fast draw and, instead, knocked the thing down the front of his pants. My pistol was in the top drawer of a desk. I reached in and grabbed it, but I was so nervous that I got my thigh in front of the desk drawer and couldn't get my hand with the pistol in it out. I yanked like mad but I was stuck. I was faced with a terrible dilemma. I could either let go of the pistol and pull my hand out of the drawer or I could keep hold of the pistol and leave my hand stuck in there. It never occurred to me to move my leg.

The invading Balto Cong were faced with one man fishing madly in his crotch and another apparently being eaten by a desk. It stopped them cold. As they stood perplexed I was struck by an inspiration. It was a wooden desk. I would simply fire through it. I flipped the safety off the .22, pointed the barrel at the Balto Cong and was just curling my finger around the trigger when the Maoists parted and there, in the line of fire, stood my airhead ex-girlfriend. 'I've come to get my ironing board and my Hermann Hesse novels,' she said, and led her companions upstairs to our former bedroom.

'It's a trap!' said Bob, extracting his gun from the bottom of a pants leg. When the Balto Cong and the ex-girlfriend came back downstairs they faced two exceedingly wide-eyed guys crouching like leopards behind an impromptu barricade of overturned book cases. They sped for the exit.

It turned out later that Bob was an undercover cop. He'd infiltrated the *Harry* collective shortly after the first issue. All his photos had been developed at the police laboratory. We'd wondered why every time we got busted for marijuana the case was dropped. Bob would always go to the District Attorney's office and convince them a trial would 'blow his cover'. It was important for him to remain undetected so he could keep his eye on . . . well, on a lot of hippie girls. Bob was in no rush to get back to the Grand Theft Auto detail. I eventually read some of the reports Bob filed with the police department. They were made up of '— — is involved in the *Harry* "scene" primarily as a means of upsetting his parents who are socially prominent,' and other such. Today, Bob is an insurance investigator in Baltimore. He's still friends with the old *Harry* staff. And, of the whole bunch of us, I believe there's only one who's far enough to the left to even be called a Democrat.

What I Believe Now

Nothing. Well, nothing much. I mean, I believe things that can be proven by reason and by experiment, and, believe you me, I want to see the logic and the lab equipment. I believe that Western civilization, after some disgusting glitches, has become almost civilized. I believe it is our first duty to protect that civilization. I believe it is our second duty to improve it. I believe it is our third duty to extend it if we can. But let's be careful about that last point. Not everybody is ready to be civilized. I wasn't in 1969.

Is There Anything to Be Gained by Re-Examining All This Nonsense?

I like to think of my behavior in the sixties as a 'learning experience'. Then again, I like to think of anything stupid I've done as a 'learning experience'. It makes me feel less stupid. However, I actually did learn one thing in the 1960s (besides how to make a hash pipe out of an empty toilet-paper roll and some aluminum foil). I learned the awful power of make-believe.

There is a deep-seated and frighteningly strong human need to make believe things are different than they are – that salamanders live forever, we all secretly have three legs and there's an enormous conspiracy somewhere which controls our every thought and deed, etc. And it's not just ignorant heathen, trying to brighten their squalid days, who think up such things. Figments of the imagination can be equally persuasive right here in clean, reasonable, education-chocked middle America. People are greedy. Life is never so full it shouldn't be fuller. What more can Shirley MacLaine, for instance, want from existence? She's already been rewarded far beyond her abilities or worth. But nothing will do until she's also been King Tut and Marie of Romania. It was this kind of hoggish appetite for epistemological romance that sent my spoiled and petulant generation on a journey to Oz, a journey from which some of us are only now straggling back, in intellectual tatters.

Many people think fantastical ideas are limited to the likes of harmonic convergences, quartz crystals that ward off cancer or, at worst, harebrained theories about who killed JFK. Unfortunately, this is not the case, especially not in this century. Two of the most fecund areas for cheap fiction are politics and economics. Which brings me to Marxism.

Marxism is a perfect example of the chimeras that fueled the sixties. And it was probably the most potent one. Albeit, much of this Marxism would have been unrecognizable to Marx. It was Marxism watered down, Marxism spiked wth LSD and Marxism adulterated with mystical food coloring. But it was Marxism nonetheless because the wildest hippie and the sternest member of the Politburo shared the same daydream, the daydream that underlies all Marxism: *that a thing might somehow be worth other than what people will give for it*. This just is not true. And any system that bases itself on such a will-o'-the-wisp is bound to fail. Communes don't work. Cuba doesn't either.

Now this might not seem like much to have learned. You may think I could have gleaned more from a half dozen years spent ruining chromosomes, morals and any chance of ever getting elected to political office. After all, the hippies are gone and – if current events are any indication – the Communists are going. But there is a part of the world where politico-economic fish stories are still greeted with gape-jawed credulity. It's a part of the world that pretty much includes everybody except us, the Japanese, some Europeans and a few of the most cynical Russians. You can call it the Third World, the Underdeveloped World or just the Part of the World That's Completely Screwed.

Over the past eight years, working as a foreign correspondent, I've spent a lot of time in the part of the world that's completely screwed. It's always seemed a comfortable and familiar-feeling place to me. The reason is, Third World countries are undergoing national adolescences very similar to the personal adolescence I underwent in the sixties. Woodstock Nation isn't dead; it's just become poor, brown, distant and filled with chaos and starvation.

Marxism has tremendous appeal in the Third World for exactly the same reason it had tremendous appeal to me in college. It gives you something to believe in when what surrounds you seems unbelievable. It gives you someone to blame besides yourself. It's theoretically tidy. And, best of all, it's fully imaginary so it can never be disproved.

The Third World attitude toward the United States is also easy to understand if you think of it in terms of adolescence. The citizens of the Third World are in a teenage muddle about us – full of envy, imitation, anger and blind puppy love. I have been held at gunpoint by a Shi'ite youth in West Beirut who told me in one breath that America was 'pig Satan devil' and that he planned to go to dental school in Dearborn as soon as he got his green card. In Ulundi, in Zululand, I talked to a young man who, as usual, blamed apartheid on the United States. However, he had just visited the US with a church group and also told me, 'Everything is so wonderful there. The race relations are so good.

And everyone is rich.' Just what part of America had he visited, I asked. 'The South Side of Chicago,' he said.

We are a beautiful twenty-year-old woman and they are a wildly infatuated thirteen-year-old boy. They think of us every moment of the day and we take no notice of them whatsoever. If they can't have a chance to love us, a chance to pester us will do – by becoming 'Communists', for example. Anything for attention.

Isn't this very like the relationship we 'dropouts' of the sixties had to the 'straight' society of our parents? Weren't we citizens of our own Underdeveloped World, the world of American teen-age pop culture?

So what are we supposed to do about all this? How do we keep the disaffected youth of the West out of mental Disney World? How do we keep the poor denizens of Africa, Asia and Latin America from embracing a myth that will make their lives even worse than they are already? How do we keep everyone from falling under the spell of some even more vile and barbaric phantom such as religious fundamentalism? We have to offer an alternative to nonsense, an alternative that is just as engaging but actually means something.

Maybe we should start by remembering that we already live in a highly idealistic, totally revolutionary society. And that our revolution is based on reality, not buncombe. Furthermore, it works. Look at America, Western Europe and Japan. It works like all hell. We have to remember it was the American Revolution, not the Bolshevik, that set the world on fire. Maybe we should start acting like we believe in that American Revolution again. This means turning our face against not only the Saddams, Qaddafis, Castros and Dengs of the world, but also against most of the US House of Representatives and half the Senate.

The President and his advisers will not have to sit up late working on a speech to fire the public in this cause. There's a perfectly suitable text already in print:

> We hold these truths to be self-evident; that all men are created equal; that they are endowed by their Creator with

certain unalienable Rights; that among these are Life, Liberty and the pursuit of Happiness; that to secure these rights, Governments are instituted among Men, deriving their just powers from the consent of the governed . . .

And that is a much wilder idea than anything which occurred to me during the 1960s.

FIDDLING
WHILE
AFRICA
STARVES

When the 'We Are the World' video first slithered into public view, I was sitting around with a friend who himself happens to be in show business. The thing gave him the willies. Me too. But neither of us could figure exactly why. 'Whenever you see people that pleased with themselves on a stage,' said my friend, 'you know you're in for a bad show.' And the USA for Africa performers did have that self-satisfied look of toddlers on a pot. But in this world of behemoth evils, such a minor lapse of taste shouldn't have upset us. We changed the channel.

Half a year later, in the middle of the Live Aid broadcast, my friend called me. 'Turn on your television,' he said. 'This is horrible. They're in a frenzy.'

'Well,' I said, 'at least it's a frenzy of charity.'

'Oh, no,' he said, 'it could be *anything*. Next time it might be "Kill the Jews."'

A mob, even an eleemosynary mob, is an ugly thing to see. No good ever came of mass emotion. The audience that's easily moved to tears is as easily moved to sadistic dementia. People are not thinking under such circumstances. And poor, dreadful Africa is something which surely needs thought.

The Band Aid, Live Aid, USA for Africa concerts and records

(and videos, posters, T-shirts, lunch buckets, thermos bottles, bath toys, etc.) are supposed to illuminate the plight of the Africans. Note the insights provided by these lyrics:

> We are the world [solipsism], *we are the*
> *children* [average age near forty]
> We are the ones to make a brighter day [unproven]
> So let's start giving [logical inference
>   supplied without argument]
> There's a choice we're making [true as far
>   as it goes]
> We're saving our own lives [absurd]
> It's true we'll make a better day [see line 2 above]
> Just you and me [statistically unlikely]

That's three palpable untruths, two dubious assertions, nine uses of a first-person pronoun, not a single reference to trouble or anybody in it and no facts. The verse contains, literally, neither rhyme nor reason.

And these musical riots of philanthropy address themselves to the wrong problems. There is, of course, a shortage of food among Africans, but that doesn't mean there's a shortage of food *in* Africa. 'A huge backlog of emergency grain has built up at the Red Sea port of Assab,' says the *Christian Science Monitor*. 'Food sits rotting in Ethiopia,' reads a headline in the *St Louis Post-Dispatch*. And according to hunger maven William Shawcross, 200,000 tons of food aid delivered to Ethiopia is being held in storage by the country's government.

There's also, of course, a lack of transport for that food, but that's not the real problem either. The authorities in Addis Ababa have plenty of trucks for their military operations against the Eritrean rebels, and much of the rest of Ethiopia's haulage is being used for forcibly resettling people instead of feeding them. Western governments are reluctant to send more trucks, for fear they'll be used the same way. And similar behavior can be seen in the rest of miserable Africa.

The African relief fad serves to distract attention from the real issues. There is famine in Ethiopia, Chad, Sudan and areas of